DIVA

A MYSTERY NOVEL BY DELACORTA

A MYSTERY NOVEL BY DELACORTA

"A lean Parisian thriller
featuring an unlikely pair of con artists;
Serge Gorodish, a failed classical pianist
who now specializes in complex crimes,
and his partner and nubile protege,
a 13-year-old kleptomaniac named Alba...
suspenseful, offbeat."
Publishers Weekly

A MYSTERY NOVEL BY DELACORTA

"DIVA, for all its sleek sophistication,
is a wonderfully old-fashioned book.
Cops and robbers, good and evil,
and true love triumphant."
Washington Post

A MYSTERY NOVEL BY DELACORTA

Translated from the French by Lowell Bair

Ballantine Books · New York

Copyright © 1979 by Editions Robert Laffont
English language translation copyright © 1983
by Summit Books, a Division of Simon & Schuster, Inc.

Library of Congress Catalog Card Number: 83-9086

ISBN 0-345-31265-1

Book design by Iris Bass

This edition published by arrangement with Summit Books

Manufactured in the United States of America

First Ballantine Books Edition: June 1984

FOR NELL, MY DIVA

DIVA

CHAPTER ONE

WHEN ALBA WALKED PAST THE WINDOW of Le Drugstore Saint-Germain in Paris, three men were eating ice cream inside. Catching sight of her, the first one nearly swallowed his spoon, the second one gulped convulsively, and the third one tossed thirty francs on the table and leaped up from his seat to run after her. What they had seen was a girl in her early teens with long blond hair and a divine body molded by a red leotard and boots.

The reason the first man nearly swallowed his spoon was that her leotard, cut low in front and back, revealed the beginnings of two delectable breasts.

The second man, more of a stickler for detail, had seen that she wore no panties or bra, and had noted the remarkable firmness of the long, smooth thigh that brushed against her big leather handbag as she walked.

Armand, her third admirer, didn't know exactly what he had seen, but it was enough to make him burst through the door like an artillery shell. Before he could hit his target, however, he was stopped on the sidewalk by a frizzy-haired woman who shoved a microphone in front of his face and announced. "Sir, I'm doing a broadcast for the *France-Culture* program. May I ask you a few questions?"

"Go right ahead," he answered with a foolish smile, his ardor suddenly wilting.

"What is a man, in your view?"

"I don't know, the opposite of a woman."

"Can you describe the man who just passed?"

"I don't know. . . . He's tall."

"You didn't notice anything else about him?"

"No."

"When you see a woman, what do you look at first?"

He thought for ten seconds, rubbing his nose, and said in an unsteady voice, "Her eyes. . . ."

"Can you describe that woman walking past the movie theater?"

"She's well built and pretty, really pretty. Curly hair, nice hips . . . and no bra? Yes, that's right, she's not wearing a bra."

"Thank you, sir," said the interviewer. She collared another customer. "What is a man, sir?"

"A man is someone who's very strong. That's the main thing."

Armand resumed his interrupted pursuit. The blond girl had stopped to look at a shop window, so it didn't take him long to catch up with her.

"You're taking a walk?" he asked, not very confident in the quality of his opening gambit.

Alba saw a veteran seducer on the wrong side of forty, handsome in his way but tired from his exploits and beginning to turn soft, like a warm caramel. The kind of man she detested.

"Yes, and you?" she said with her most guileless smile.

"Me too. Can I take you to a movie?"

Alba stopped, looked at her watch, and said sorrowfully, "Too bad, I don't have time."

"Then how about listening to some music in my car? It's right over there in that parking garage."

"Do you have any good rock 'n' roll?"

"Of course."

"All right, then. I just have to get something in the pharmacy. Will you wait for me here?"

"Sure," he said eagerly.

He saw her walk back toward Le Drugstore. It took him a moment to realize that besides selling food, books, and a motley array of other articles, Le Drugstore was also a pharmacy. What could that little slut have to buy in a pharmacy? He waited several minutes, traveling in the future.

When she returned, he took her into the garage and down to the lower level where his Chrysler-Simca was parked. He didn't bother to open its door for her.

"You're a very beautiful girl," he said while he fumbled with his cassettes.

He put on a tape of the Frères Jacques. Their syrupy harmony brought a look of disgust to Alba's face. She opened her bag, took out the big black plastic pistol she had just bought in Le Drugstore, and, using the two-handed grip she had seen in the movies, pointed it at Armand's chest. He shrank away from her in terror.

"Hand over your money, you fat pig, or I'll blow you away," Alba said calmly.

His trembling made it hard for him to get his wallet out of his pocket. He counted the hundred-franc bills. There were twelve of them. When he reached into another pocket for his ten-franc bills, Alba snapped, "Keep your small change for your daughter. Go buy her a leotard. She'll like it and so will you."

She grabbed the money, got out of the car, and disappeared.

A quarter of an hour later, Alba was strolling from store to store in the Tour Montparnasse, window-shopping and thinking fondly of Serge Gorodish. They had met in the small town near Paris where she was born. He had come there to get his bearings and make plans for giving his life a new direction. The moment she saw him step off the train in the dingy station she knew he wasn't like other men. He was tall and about forty, with dark, deep-set eyes, short hair and a fascinating, Asian-looking face. She had watched him walk past, he stared at her a second, and something clicked between them.

One day they came face-to-face and recognized that each was the indispensable complement of the other's nature. Serge Gorodish had age and experience. Alba had freshness, ambition, reckless-ness, intelligence, sensitivity, and a total lack of scruples. Her thirteen-year-old face was a captivating mask behind which fantastic plans were concocted.

She was impressed by Serge's talents. He had done a little of everything. After starting out as a baker's helper, he had taken up the piano—serious music, like Rachmaninoff—and practiced ten hours a day till the age of twenty-three. Then, having decided that his chances of making a living in classical music were too slim, he played the piano in bars till he crossed over to the other side of the law by becoming a gangster's chauffeur. After a time, he quit that job and supported himself by drawing cartoons and taking "artistic" photographs of young girls (very young, too young for the law) till the day when he took a train to Alba's hometown.

A kind of frenzied excitement quickly sprang up between them. Serge ferreted out her fellow citizens' guilty secrets and smoldering hostilities and used them to stir up so much trouble that the quiet little town was thrown into violent turmoil, with people insulting, attacking, and even killing each other. He then took advantage of the commotion to walk out of a bank with nine hundred and fifty thousand francs of its depositors' money. Only Alba knew who was behind the chaos.

It was time to go, and he wanted to take Alba with him. Aided by the argument of money, he convinced her father that such a gifted child needed a guardian who could further her development.

Serge and Alba left together and went to stay in his country house, the only thing he had really cared about before he met her. It was a beautiful house in the middle of spacious grounds with magnificent trees. He had always gone there whenever he needed to calm down, play the piano, and get in touch with the wisest part of himself. In that house, he and Alba would have time to think over what they wanted to do next.

They had now decided to live in Paris.

Jules started off on his motorbike. The excitement that showed in his face made him look even younger than his nineteen years. He didn't care about the light rain, or anything else, as he zigzagged through traffic on his way to the Théâtre des Champs-Elysées to attend the first European concert of the black soprano Cynthia Hawkins, a super-Diva whose voice had enraptured the American critics. The house had been sold out three days after tickets went on sale.

Jules leaned his bike against a tree. Several hundred devoted fans were standing in line, hoping they could somehow get tickets. Jules unfastened the straps that held his violin case on the baggage rack and went inside. He worked as a messenger for RCA and had gotten his ticket from Myriam, in the public-relations department. For her, he would have delivered records to China.

The lobby was full of mink-clad old ladies with reconditioned faces, slowly drifting around like decrepit goldfish showing off their flabby, spotted fins.

Jules recognized everyone who counted in the Paris musical world. The heads of all the record companies' Artists and Repertory departments were there. He grimaced when he caught sight of a music critic who just didn't like beautiful voices, a man with the face of a piranha who poisoned the airwaves once a week with his vitriol and had a wife who sang like a gurgling drainpipe, which everyone knew but no one dared say.

Jules made his way across the lobby, avoiding the sharks and barracudas. Among them floated a few starry-eyed, frail young men who turned to quivering jelly at the sound of an unfaltering high C.

Jules bought a program, then tried to blot out the mediocrity around him. The image of an aquarium faded from his mind and was replaced by a vision of the Diva whose picture dominated the front page of the program.

The ushers' faces fell halfway to their knees when they saw him come into the two-hundred-franc orchestra seats wearing jeans and a brown leather flight jacket that showed clear signs of having had hard use for a good quarter of a century.

His seat was in the center of the third row. He stepped on a few expensive shoes in the process of getting to the seat, then slowly sat down in it as if he were easing himself into a bathtub. The people around him were vigorously whispering to each other. He waited till they had forgotten him before standing his violin case on end between his legs. There was no violin in his case. It contained a Nagra tape recorder with the best microphones he could find: Shoeps. He had spent weeks putting together and improving his ingenious setup. The tape recorder could be turned on with a switch in the handle of the case. The balance was preset according to the acoustics of the hall, his position in it, and the kind of instrument he wanted to record.

Over the last five years he had built up a unique collection of live recordings. Whenever he wished, he could summon up divas to reproduce the most sublime moments of their concerts. A technician at Deutsche Grammophon in Hamburg had been astounded by the quality of a tape that Jules had let him hear, a recital by Leontyne Price at the Paris Opéra. Jules poured all his money into that powerful, absorbing passion. He knew singing as well as if he had been nursed by a soprano whose breasts produced liquid music.

He looked up at the ceiling painted by Maurice Denis in 1910. Pastel colors that would make Andy Warhol choke. The fat, pink Muses floated blissfully in a pale sky, naked except for wisps of cloth that saved them from indecency. Jules wished they would piss on the chattering bourgeois audience below them.

He focused his attention on the empty stage where

the Steinway glowed like a black pearl. The multiple faces of his Diva, whose photographs he had cut out of the American magazines he subscribed to, began swirling in his head and making electric quivers run through his body.

He made sure the microphones hidden in the upper part of his violin case were correctly aimed at the stage, and then, since the concert was late in starting, he looked over the biography of Cynthia Hawkins in the program. She was born in Alabama. The year wasn't given, but Jules knew she was thirty-two. First recital at Carnegie Hall in 1975. Horlick, the toughest critic in the West, wrote in *The New York Times*: "...the magic of a voice that reaches the sublime and holds you spellbound from note to note to the point of rapture." Debut at the Metropolitan Opera two years later, in the role of Donna Anna. Her performance was followed by an ovation that lasted forty-three minutes. Other roles: Tosca, Pamina, Lulu, Leonora, Aida, Tatiana, Lucia, Carmen.

In spite of all the offers that had been made to her, Cynthia Hawkins steadfastly refused to make any recordings or appear on radio or television. This helped to make each of her performances a unique and exciting event. She also refused to give more than twenty concerts a season because, she said, it was impossible for her to die more than twice a month.

Spotlights, silence. The lid of the piano reflected golden light against the back of the stage. More waiting. Then the little door on the left opened and Cynthia Hawkins appeared in a magnificent red gown slit up to her thigh. Her hair was like a halo above her full, sensuous face, which showed a trace of anxiety. Jules turned on his tape recorder. The pianist began a Schubert lied. The Diva's voice penetrated Jules' body and the first tears flowed down his cheeks. He was inside the music.

After three days of looking, Serge and Alba had been shown a superb apartment with eight rooms, a terrace, and a private elevator, on the top floor of a building at the corner of the Rue de l'Université and the Rue de Beaune. Serge had said yes to it immediately.

Now he was alone in the empty apartment. The sound of the intercom jolted him out of his daydreams. Alba came in with a man behind her. Each of them dropped an armload of packages on the floor.

"Serge, this is Mohammed. He's been supernice to me. His taxi was stuffed full of things I bought. He stayed with me all afternoon."

Serge shook hands with the Berber cabdriver. He had a likable face.

"Do you have a phone?" Serge asked him.

"Yes, why?"

"We'll be doing a lot of traveling around the city, so if you're free..."

"I'll be free when you need me."

"*Wakha*" said Serge, showing off one of the few Arabic words he knew. "Come by tomorrow morning at ten o'clock. We'll go shopping. We still need things."

They emptied two bottles of Chinese beer while Alba sipped a Coke. Serge gave Mohammed the money for her fare, plus a big tip, and then he was alone with his tempting angel.

She kissed him on the corner of the lips and began unwrapping packages to show him the results of her shopping expedition.

There were two red sleeping bags, inflatable mattresses, blankets, pillows, a Chinese thermos bottle, an Italian designer lamp, coffee, sugar, milk, cups, silverware, plates, glasses, and banana Nesquik.

"Not bad for a start, right?"

"It's perfect."

"I went to a big department store called the Samaritaine. It's a terrific place, full of all kinds of stuff I'd love to steal."

"You can have one of the rooms to store your loot in, but first we have to turn this place into a livable apartment. It will take us at least a week."

"What's wrong with it now? We've got sleeping bags, the plumbing works, the phone is connected—what else do you want? There's already a big rug, so all we need is a lot of cushions to put on it. We'll live on the floor. I've always wanted to do that."

"Listen, this is an apartment, not a campsite," laughed Gorodish.

He sized up the dimensions of the room and imagined shelves of records, a first-rate stereo, and himself, stretched out on a sofa—or on cushions, it didn't matter—listening. . . .

The first notes of Beethoven's Diabelli Variations came into his head. It was a piece he had worked long and hard on, years ago. While he was floating in the ethereal realm of music, Alba went into the kitchen to make herself a huge glass of banana Nesquik. She drank half of it and came back to him.

"I want a darkroom," she said. "We'll have at least one spare room we can use for it. Will you teach me to make pictures?"

"If you like. But before we start thinking about your darkroom, we've got to buy beds, chairs, and a table."

"What do you think this is, some kind of warehouse? We're lucky enough to get a big, empty apartment and all you can think of is cramming it full of useless junk. The only thing you really need is a good stereo for listening to your Rachmaninoff. We'll get along fine on the floor, believe me."

"People think better when they're comfortable," Gorodish said with an amused smile. "But why don't we compromise? We'll get a lot of cushions so you can make yourself at home on the floor, and a good leather sofa for me."

"That suits me. We can both have our own space."

Alba opened the big glass doors and stepped out onto the terrace. She loved that terrace. She imagined it with a forest alongside it, so she could see trees when she woke up in the morning.

She wished Serge would put a little more passion into their discussions. He was always so calm and unflappable, while she dreamed of stormy quarrels followed by tender repentance and amorous reconciliations.

She decided to try a new strategy.

"We'll sleep in a big bed, in a bedroom, with a mirror and everything. You don't have to worry about me getting pregnant because I'll go on the pill."

"Forget it. You'll just have to keep your virginity a little longer. You'll have your own bedroom, with your own sleeping bag and cot."

"You mean we're not going to sleep together?"

"That's right."

"It's my age, isn't it?" she asked sulkily.

"Wait till you're fourteen. Right now, we've got other things to do together. Planning big jobs, for example."

Alba's face brightened.

"That's what I like to hear. I got rid of one father and I don't want another one. I fell in love with you because you weren't like anyone else I knew. Your clothes weren't so great, but your eyes turned me on. . . . I don't care about luxury, except for one thing: I want a big round bathtub, like the ones Hollywood stars have."

"It's yours."

"A round bathtub and a darkroom, that's all I want."

"Then there's nothing for us to argue about. You don't want a car too?"

"Haven't you heard about taxis and subways?"

Gorodish nodded and was silent for a few moments.

"Alba, I'm starting to get an idea about something . . ."

"Something that will make us a lot of money?"

"I think so."

"Tell me about it. Maybe I can help you plan it."

"Not now. It needs to simmer a little longer."

"Just think of it, Serge: if I hadn't met you, I'd still be rotting in that stupid little town. I always dreamed of having a life like this, so free, so much fun . . . I'm starving. Let's go out and get something to eat."

They left for the restaurant. The rain had stopped. They walked along, holding hands. She wanted to go into a pizzeria and he let her take him there.

The concert had just ended. After the third encore, Jules hurried backstage. He was one of the first to arrive. The door of the little dressing room was closed. While the Diva kept her admirers waiting, their number grew till there was a crowd in front of the door. Jules recognized a friend of his who ran a record store and gave him discounts, a wild and wonderful blond woman with a knowledge of opera second to none. They were both so overcome with emotion that they couldn't speak.

At last the door opened and the admirers poured in to pay homage to their sublime idol.

She had changed clothes. A beautiful black dress with a low, diamond-studded neckline had replaced her fiery red gown, which was now casually draped over a chair.

Jules struggled to hold back his tears. Cynthia Hawkins gave him a gracious smile and autographed his program. He stood in front of her, captivated, till other admirers pushed him aside. The red gown was right next to him. Scarcely aware of what he was doing, he took hold of it by one sleeve, gently pulled it toward him, rolled it up and put it under his leather jacket. Then he left the dressing room after taking one last look at his Diva.

He went out with the others, passed the guard at the stage entrance, and rode off on his motorbike, elated and triumphant. With the gown still next to him under his jacket, he happily sped along the streets, his ears and his body full of music.

Bellowing fragments of lieder into the night, he rode till he came to the building in the Twentieth Arrondissement where he had a studio apartment overlooking the outer boulevards.

He put on a record of Strauss's *Four Last Songs*, turned up the volume, tossed his jacket into a corner, and stretched out on the mattress that lay directly on the floor. He kept the Diva's gown against him and breathed in the delightful fragrance that still permeated it. He was in the grip of a divine madness.

Jean Saporta wasn't Louis XIV, but his isolated and well-guarded little Versailles, in the Paris suburb of Beauvais, always left visitors gaping. The heated pool, the Turkish bath, the billiard room, the paintings by eighteenth-century minor masters, the Chinese cook, even the silence—everything gave an impression of money and order.

Nadia belonged to Saporta, as one object among others. She was there to shine, and she put up a shining appearance. It was night now. Lights were on all over the silent house. Saporta was away.

Nadia felt she couldn't go on any longer. Behind all the luxury around her, she saw the little bags of heroin that Saporta supplied to France. Saporta was a drug and prostitution magnate, as others were sugar or steel magnates. Nadia was a product of his business empire. She had begun at the bottom, as one of his zealous workers, then he had singled her out and promoted her. Now that she was twenty-seven, her age was becoming a handicap. A whole crowd of younger women intent on replacing her were already jockeying for position. Saporta did her the honor of tolerating her, but for some time she had felt that the end of her precarious reign was approaching.

Saporta hadn't spoken to her in three weeks. A few curt words had greeted her return to life after she tried to kill herself by cutting her wrists: "Noboby commits suicide without my permission. Remember that."

She kept repeating these words to herself. Saporta wouldn't deign to use a repaired object. He couldn't even stand a retouched painting, much less a woman who had been cut open and sewn back together. What was he going to do with her? At best, give her permission to die. Or maybe he would sell her.

She had once heard him proudly talk about handing over one of his mistresses to an Iraqi friend.

The only difference between Nadia and the others was that in two years she had carefully gathered important information, thinking at first that it might someday bring her enough money to last the rest of her life. She had quickly realized that trying to blackmail Saporta wouldn't work, but she had continued to keep her eyes and ears open.

Her reasoning was simple. Saporta ruled through fear. She was no longer afraid because she accepted death. Saporta was therefore at her mercy.

Her plan had been ready a long time.

She went up to her room, turned on her tape recorder, and began making the cassette that would put an end to Saporta's career.

In a quavering voice, she described his organization in precise detail and pointed out all the ramifications she knew about, in both prostitution and heroin. Then she cited people by name, including the corrupt policeman who had been covering Saporta.

After fifty minutes of methodical work, Nadia stopped, with her throat dry, gasping for breath, terrified at the thought of the process she had just set in motion. She hid the cassette in a drawer full of underwear and lay down on her bed, hoping Saporta wouldn't stop her from going out the next day.

Since she didn't have much faith in luck, she wasn't yet ready to rejoice, but a deep, inexplicable feeling of strength was rising inside her. She exultantly imagined Saporta ending his days in a prison cell, abandoned by everyone, weak, paying for his crimes at last.

Late in the night, she heard his Mercedes crunching the gravel of the driveway. He went up to his room without stopping by to see her.

Alba unrolled the sleeping bags.

"I hope you don't mind if we sleep next to each other till we get beds," she said.

Serge preferred to change the subject: "Next time I'll take you to a good restaurant."

"You didn't like the one we went to tonight?"

"It was all right."

He slid into his sleeping bag. Alba took a long shower. He watched her come in naked and wet.

"We don't even have a towel," she complained. "Tomorrow I'll buy some big ones."

"Dry yourself with your shirt and put it on the radiator."

He couldn't help contemplating the smooth surfaces and harmonious curves of the body he adored.

She turned off the light, got into the bag, nestled her head against his shoulder, and quickly fell asleep. He kissed her lightly on the lips.

CHAPTER TWO

JULES PUT THE LATEST *HOROWITZ ALBUM IN*-to the saddlebag of his motorbike. Behind the windshield he had attached a little cigar box to hold his cassette player. The air was softer today, as if autumn were about to give way to spring. Clumps of white clouds were drifting across the sky. Jules liked his work because it gave him a feeling of freedom.

As he skillfully wove in and out of traffic, not wearing a helmet because he couldn't bear to have his ears blocked, he was totally absorbed in the pure voice of Leontyne Price floating back to him from the cassette player. This morning she was singing Carmen. He was on his way to Radio-France to deliver the Horowitz album. Instead of going along the Seine, he headed for the Avenue de la Grande-Armée to have a drink with the other messengers who gathered in a café there. Those who were paid on a piecework basis often traded assignments with each other so they could group their deliveries in one neighborhood and do more of them in a day. Jules was paid a monthly salary and made all his assigned deliveries himself. He always dealt with the same people and he liked them, because he was passionately interested in anything that concerned music.

In his pocket was the little embroidered handkerchief he had found in his Diva's red gown. Knowing she was staying at the Ritz, he planned to pass by there, on the chance that he might be lucky enough to see her.

Mohammed arrived at ten o'clock, as agreed. Alba, who had just gotten up, gave him a cup of coffee. Gorodish had been up a long time. After buying two newspapers, *Metro* and *Libération*, he had gone to Pan-Musique, on the Rue Jacob, and listened to several stereos. He had finally decided on a Technics, with Elipson speakers. A technician was to come and install it that afternoon.

Gorodish seemed a little distracted, as if he were meditating about something.

"Where shall we start?" asked Alba.

"What's your choice?"

"I'd like to go back to the Galeries Lafayette to buy the pots and pans and all the other stuff for the kitchen."

"I'd rather get a sofa, a bed, and a table."

"Then come with me to the Galaries Lafayette. They have furniture too."

"All right."

Mohammed handled his taxi gently, like a chauffeur driving a limousine.

Two hours later, Serge and Alba began unwrapping things and putting them away. He had given her free rein and she seemed to have done quite well. All he had bought was a bed. For the rest, he would go to the luxury shops on the Boulevard Saint-Germain that afternoon. They would probably have what he was looking for.

This time Alba wanted to have lunch at Le Drugstore, because of the ice cream.

A little before eleven o'clock when Nadia had her breakfast brought to her in bed, she learned that Saporta had already left.

Half an hour later she got into her Lancia and began driving to Paris. After making sure she wasn't being followed, she stopped at a phone booth. The only man she could safely ask to help her was Michel Krantz, one of her former lovers, a private detective who wasn't very good at his work but was scrupulously honest. She dialed his office number.

"Hello, Michel . . ."

"Who's this?"

"It's me, Nadia."

"Why are you calling me? Is anything wrong?"

"I've got something very important for you. Information. On a cassette. I want you to give it to someone reliable."

"I don't like that kind of thing very much. . . . But for you, I'll risk it."

"Shall I bring the cassette to your apartment?"

"No. I've moved. I live in Sceaux now, and it's too complicated to explain how to get there. If you like, we can meet at the Dupont-Wagram for lunch, in an hour."

"I'll be there."

At the Ritz, panic had reigned since the night before. As she was about to go to the hotel restaurant, where a group of music critics and record company executives were waiting for her, the Diva had discovered that her red gown was missing. Several people had hurried back to the theater to look for it, in vain.

Violently upset, Cynthia Hawkins had refused to leave her suite at the Ritz. Even without the loss of her gown, she would have felt too emotionally drained to answer the critics' questions and politely reject the offers of the record companies. She had given the public everything she had to give that evening. It was perhaps the best performance of her life.

Her red gown was the one she had worn for her first recital, and then for other occasions that had always turned out successfully for her. She was terrified at the thought of confronting the London public in two weeks, wearing a new gown. She was ready to cancel the concert. She had spent a sleepless night, as she always did after a concert, but this time she had the added stress of vainly waiting for word that her gown had been found.

In the morning, she couldn't hold back her tears when Simon Weinstadt, her agent, came in and proudly showed her the headline on the front page of *France-Soir:* WHO STOLE THE DIVA'S GOWN? He opened *Le Figaro, Le Matin,* and *Le Quotidien de Paris*, in which the reviews of the concert were rhapsodic. He knew that the review in *Le Monde* would be equally satisfactory. Only one article panned Cynthia Hawkins. Its title was "The Coca-Cola Diva" (which was insulting to both the soft drink and singer, since they were both like dark champagne), and it was written by the piranha-faced critic Jules had seen in the lobby. Luckily, that vicious idiot didn't write for an important paper.

Weinstadt didn't show the article to Cynthia.

To make amends for her absence the night before, she had promised to give a press conference that afternoon, and reporters were beginning to arrive in the salons of the Ritz.

Michel Krantz was sitting at a round table in one corner of the Dupont-Wagram. Nadia barely recognized him when she came in. He looked tired, worn out. He smiled at her, but his face was bitter. She was a little ashamed of her own appearance, knowing it had been marked by her life with Saporta.

"You've changed," she said.

"You and I have moved in opposite directions."

"Not lately. I think we're both at the same point now."

"I'm glad to see you again."

"You're the only person I trust."

"I'm surprised to hear that, since you must know a lot of people," Krantz said sarcastically.

"Yes, but you know what kind of people they are."

"Tell me about the cassette you want to give me. Is it really important, like you said?"

"It's dynamite. If it gets into the right hands, it'll put Saporta away for good."

"Why are you doing this?"

"Because I can't take any more," Nadia said with a deep sigh.

"I've already talked to someone who's very reliable. Within a few hours, the wheels will start rolling."

"Thanks."

"Do you want me to make sure you're safe?"

"You know there's no way I can be safe. They'd find me no matter where I went. And I'm finished anyway."

"You're giving up," said Krantz, his face sagging.

"I gave up long ago."

"Let me try to get you out of this. Stay with me. There's no one else in my life."

"It would only be a reprieve. You don't know Saporta."

"But I know what he's like. . . . Listen, I'm not hungry and I think it'll be better if we separate right now."

Nadia gave him the cassette, took one last look at him, left him, and began driving back to Beauvais.

She stopped twice, and opened the windows of the car to try to breathe normally.

Chang, Saporta's Chinese cook, was on pins and needles. He had vital information for his boss, but couldn't get in touch with him. Once again he tried the number of the Mercedes. This time, Saporta answered.

"What is it?"

"Something urgent, sir, urgent! I got a phone call from someone who works at the Dupont-Wagram in Paris. He recognized Nadia there. She met a man named Krantz and gave him a cassette."

"Has she come back yet?"

"No, sir."

"If she gets there before I do, don't let her leave for any reason."

"I'll keep her here, sir."

Saporta hung up.

"Take me home, Louis. Fast."

* * *

Alba had eaten a peach Melba and a dish of ice cream with bilberry liqueur. Gorodish wanted to stay in the neighborhood but she felt like exploring. She walked up the Boulevard Saint-Germain, crossed the Place de la Concorde, and began strolling along the Champs-Elysées in the direction of the Arc de Triomphe.

When she came to Lido-Musique, she went inside. She wanted to give Serge a record. She went down to the basement and looked around, undecided.

She stopped in front of a picture of the South American pianist, Jorge Bolet. An album of Liszt concert studies. She had a sudden impulse to steal it. A saleswoman was talking with a young man in a leather jacket. They didn't seem to be paying any attention to Alba. The hard part would be leaving after she went back to the first floor. She deftly slipped the record under her poncho and climbed the stairs. The first floor was crowded. She casually drifted toward the door and went out. No one called after her.

She walked ten paces and looked back. She had gotten away with it. Serge would be pleased. No use paying for records when you could get them free.

Jules cut short his conversation with the saleswoman. He had seen Alba leave with her record, and admired her slick performance. When he came out of the store, he saw her blond hair in the distance. He got on his motorbike and caught up with her, riding between the startled pedestrians on the sidewalk.

"Don't be afraid, I don't work for the store. I'm a messenger. You like classical music?"

"Of course, otherwise I'd steal disco records."

"You might have gotten caught."

"Is that a tape recorder hanging from your neck?"

"Yes. I like to work with music."

"Is it an expensive one?"

"Pretty expensive, yes."

"Did you steal it?" Alba asked with a smile.

"No. I spend all my money on music."

"I like to steal things. Even if I have money on me."

"What's your name?"

"Alba. What's yours?"

"Jules."

"What an old-fashioned name."

"I'd like to give you a record. I work for RCA. They have a tremendous catalog of opera and a lot of other things. Do you like opera?"

"I don't know much about it. Mainly I like piano music."

"I have to go now because I've got something that's supposed to be delivered in a hurry and I'm already late, but how about meeting me tomorrow? I'll give you the record."

"Okay, where shall we meet?"

"In front of Lido-Musique. I'll have some free time at noon. Can you meet me at twelve-thirty for lunch?"

"Sure. See you tomorrow, Jules."

"So long, Alba."

She watched him ride away. She liked him. He had brown curly hair, a rather triangular face, and dark, lively eyes, and he wasn't pretentious. Alba didn't like the student type. She was glad she had met Jules because he worked and his job seemed interesting to her.

* * *

Paula was a police inspector, one of the best members of the Vice Squad. When Krantz had called her, she had realized immediately that this could be the biggest thing she had ever handled in her career. As she walked toward the Champs-Elysées on her way to meet Krantz, she wondered if what was on that cassette was really enough to put a man as wily as Saporta behind bars. Krantz had seemed to think so and, considering how anxious he was to get rid of the cassette, Paula was inclined to believe it was true.

She went into the movie house after checking the title of the film: Kubrick's *Barry Lyndon*. She was exactly on time. It took her eyes a little while to adjust to the darkness. She counted three rows from the back, spotted Krantz's light tan coat and sat down beside him. A duel on a riverbank. When the shot was fired, Krantz handed her the cassette. She put it in the pocket of her raincoat. He waited a few minutes before leaving. Paula stayed till the end of the film, then hailed a taxi on the Champs-Elysées. A short time later she was in her apartment on the Avenue Bosquet. She made herself a cup of coffee.

She had decided to keep the cassette till the next morning. She would have to make sure she gave it to the right person because she knew Saporta had accomplices in high places.

Her face, surrounded by curly chestnut hair, was tense. A fine line marked her high forehead. She prepared a bath for herself and plunged into the blue suds. A bathtub was her favorite place for making big decisions. She thought of the Christmas vacation she would spend in Marrakesh, alone or with the man of the moment.

An hour later she had decided to give the cassette

to Boulanger, the head of the Vice Squad. There was no reason to let Narcotics have it first, since a quarter of all the high-class prostitutes in Paris worked for Saporta.

Nadia was surprised to see the Mercedes in front of the house when she arrived. She went into the living room. Saporta was standing there. He was a short, wiry man whose strength was concentrated in his dark face with eyes that never seemed to move; even his eyelids gave the impression that they never blinked. He wore only double-breasted suits made of the finest fabrics, with slightly padded shoulders. His short gray hair was carefully combed and divided by an impeccable part on the left side. It was when he smiled that he looked most ferocious. Not one of his features moved.

Nadia realized that she was lost. She trembled.

"I told you not to see Krantz again. Tell me exactly what's on that cassette."

Nadia couldn't get any words out of her throat. Louis was sitting in a corner, flipping the pages of a magazine.

"Well? What's on it?"

"Everything."

"Explain."

"Everything I know. The organization. The heroin, and all the rest."

Nadia spoke like a robot. She felt as if she were already dead. She had almost stopped being afraid.

"What's Krantz's address?"

"He lives in Sceaux. That's all I can tell you; I don't know the address."

"Louis, put her in the cellar. We'll take care of her later."

Louis grabbed Nadia and shoved her down the

stairs. She found herself in a cement cubicle, behind a steel door, surprised to still be alive.

When Jules discovered the article in *France-Soir*, his love for the Diva spurred him into action. He rode home, took the red gown and the handkerchief, and headed for the Ritz.

The lobby was full of reporters. Jules had the gown under his jacket. He spoke to the man at the reception desk, who looked at him as if he had asked to see the pope.

"All these gentlemen have been waiting a long time. Miss Hawkins isn't receiving any visitors."

Jules asked for an envelope, put the Diva's handkerchief in it, and had it taken to her.

A minute later, a bellhop led him to her suite. He went in through the door marked 212.

His heart was pounding like Bartók's sonata for two pianos and percussion. He waited in the drawing room, standing. He was still trying to think of what he would say when the Diva came in. She recognized him immediately.

"I have your gown, Miss Hawkins," he said quickly.

"You want money?"

"No, not at all." He opened his jacket. "Here it is. I'm sorry it's a little wrinkled."

"Why have you brought it to me?"

"I read the article in the paper. I realized it was more important for you than for me."

"I appreciate your kindness. Sit down. Would you like something to drink?"

"No, please don't bother. . . ."

"Do you like tea?"

"Yes. . . ."

Cynthia Hawkins picked up the phone and ordered two teas. Jules couldn't believe what was happening to him. He felt that his face had turned scarlet. He wished that time would make a long pause so he could savor these moments better. He hoped the tea would be very slow in coming. She was there in front of him, wearing a shimmering blue-green dress made from Indian silk. The room was filled with the smell of her perfume. This was happiness raised to the tenth power. She sat down facing him.

"Your concert last night was... I don't know how to tell you..."

"Don't try to think of words, they're always the same. I understand better from seeing people's faces, and when I saw yours last night, I understood."

"I never know what to say at times like that....I know everything you've done, or at least everything written about you in American magazines."

"I see you're a real fan!" she said in English.

The sight of his Diva's smile brought Jules' emotional circuits dangerously close to an overload. He was speechless. All he could do was look at her.

A bellhop brought in a tray and left. She poured a cup of tea for Jules—she, Cynthia Hawkins, the Diva, pouring him a cup of tea!

"I...I hope the wrinkles will come out of your gown," he stammered.

"Did you sleep with it?"

"No. Well, not really."

"I want to give you a present."

"A present? For me?"

"Come."

He stood up. She took him by the hand and led him into her bedroom. Things were scattered all over it: empty mineral-water bottles, a tray on the

bed, clothes tossed at random, an open suede suitcase.

She opened the door of a wardrobe with a wall
lamp above it. There were at least thirty dresses
hanging in it, showing a wide range of colors. There
were also shoes, scarves, a black mink coat, black
like Cynthia, and another coat made of fur from a
kind of animal Jules had seen at the circus, either
a tiger or a leopard.

"Take any dress you want."

"You really mean it?"

"Yes. You can choose and keep it."

"I can't; I'd rather have you choose one for me."

"If you like."

Cynthia's slender hands moved along the multi-
colored dresses. She took out a long pearl-gray gown
decorated with a band of embroidery on a matching
background that slanted across the bodice and had
a diamond at its lower end.

"Do you want this one? I've often worn it when
I sang."

She handed him the gown. They went back into
the drawing room. He was speechless again, beside
himself with joy. His throat was so tight that he
could scarcely swallow his tea. The phone rang.
Cynthia promised to come downstairs immediately.

"That was my agent, Simon Weinstadt. The reporters are waiting for me. I have to go."

"How long will you stay in Paris?"

"At least ten days. My next concert is on No-
vember eighth, in London."

"What will you sing?"

"Schubert, Wolf, Fauré."

Jules had finished his cup of tea. He stood up,
carefully folded the pearl-gray gown and put it un-

der his jacket. Suddenly he felt something rising from his entrails into his throat. He pressed his lips together, trying to restrain himself, but his eyes filled with tears. Cynthia opened the door. She took him by the shoulders, still with that magic smile, and kissed him on the cheeks.

"Call me tomorrow morning at ten, all right?"

Jules nodded and turned away to hide the fountain that had begun gushing in his eyes.

In the elevator, he put on his sunglasses. As he hurried across the lobby he waved to Gallo, who was talking with the head of Nippon Columbia's A & R department and one of his assistants. The two Japanese looked at Jules with what seemed to be anxiety.

"Who's that?" asked Tsukahara.

"A messenger for RCA," answered Gallo. "He loves opera."

"He was visiting Miss Hawkins. We hope she is not negotiating an agreement with our honorable colleagues."

"They wouldn't have sent a messenger to negotiate for them."

"Who knows? The end justifies the means," said the Japanese, proud of himself for having come up with this expression.

The arrival of the glorious Diva put an end to the conversation.

Jules was on his motorbike, heading for home. His work would have to wait. He felt as if he were on a flying carpet.

A malicious cabdriver cut him off and he had to go up onto the sidewalk to avoid a spill. Cabdrivers were the messenger's implacable enemy. After some imaginative swearing, Jules continued on his way.

As soon as he was in his apartment he turned on his amplifier and looked over the fiberboard shelves holding several hundred recordings of operatic music.

The Célestion Ditton 66 speakers stood out darkly in the twelve-by-sixteen-foot room. On one wall were photographs of the greatest singers. In the middle of them appeared his Diva, represented by a large black-and-white portrait reproduced from a picture in an American magazine. A pearl necklace glowed against the background of her dark skin. Jules looked at her fascinating mouth for several moments.

The floor was speckled with spots of different colors. A painter had lived in the apartment before Jules. In one corner, beside a small refrigerator, was a rickety table with a two-burner gas camping stove and a few kitchen utensils. Jules took a strawberry yogurt from the refrigerator and stretched out comfortably on the mattress that served as his bed. His clothes were stuffed into the record cabinets that still had some extra room in them. He had made allowance for a large record collection, but it was obvious that he would soon have to put up more shelves.

The miraculous tape was on his Nagra. He pushed the switch, recognized the silence of the Théâtre des Champs-Elysées, and took a deep breath. The piano began, and then came the Diva's voice in all its splendor and controlled intensity. The speakers marvelously reproduced its texture, the slightest fluctuations of timbre, the breathing, the pure, almost ethereal vibrato. The subtleties of the lied flowed into him like a river. The piano was clear and neither too loud nor too soft. Everything was perfect.

Jules forgot the world. He was totally absorbed in the music, suspended in space, intoxicated by the sensual perfume of his Diva's pearl-gray gown.

MICHEL KRANTZ HAD SPENT THE EVE-ning playing cards with friends. When a taxi dropped him in front of his little house, the fruit of a lifetime of hard work without much success, it was nearly three in the morning.

In the garden, he took a melancholy glance at the hull of the small sailboat he had been building from plans sent to him by a boating magazine. Either the plans were drawn by a half-wit or Krantz had no talent for do-it-yourself projects. He knew his boat would never reach the sea but he kept it anyway because he had worked on it every weekend since the first warm days of spring and he didn't want to waste an equal amount of time undoing what he had done.

He had thought about Nadia all evening. He could hardly believe she had once been his mistress. A woman like her, with him ... That bastard Saporta had ruined her, destroyed her. She had given

Krantz the feeling that there was nothing left inside her; that was how he described it to himself, and the expression seemed apt to him.

As he walked along the row of little concrete slabs that led to his house, he called his cat, who usually went out in the evening.

"Here, Toto. Here, Toto. Come and see your papa."

Well, after all, Toto could sleep in the garage if he wanted to. Since he hadn't come, he must have found something to eat. Krantz called him once again. He was used to sleeping with his cat.

He went into the house, turned on the light, and gasped. Saporta and his guardian angels were sitting in the living room. Something that looked very much like a .38 with a silencer was pointing at Krantz, and Toto was there, on Saporta's lap. Cats are odd.

"This is a pretty shabby place you've got here, Krantz. I told you a few years ago that you didn't look like somebody who'd ever succeed in life. Do you think we're going to kill you?"

They didn't waste any time, thought Krantz. He secretly admired Saporta's efficiency. It wasn't for nothing that he stayed at the head of his empire while everyone who gave him any trouble wound up lying in a coffin.

"What do you want?"

"We wanted to wish you a Happy New Year," said Paulo, the one holding the gun. He wasn't noted for his refinement. Saporta had more class.

"You've got a chance to get out of this in one piece," said Saporta. "Don't blow it. Where's the cassette?"

"I got rid of it. It was too hot for me to handle."

"You should have thought of that first. What did you do with it?"

"As soon as Nadia called me, I called a police inspector I know, in the Vice Squad. I met her an hour after I saw Nadia, and gave her the cassette."

"You didn't even take time to listen to it?"

"No. I didn't want to get mixed up in this."

"That's what's wrong with you: no ambition. Let's have your inspector's name and address."

"What if I won't tell you?"

Paulo chuckled good-naturedly. "Don't joke with us, pal, we're tired. We're not used to working at night."

"All right, all right. She's Paula Dumézil, Sixty-four Avenue Bosquet."

"Do you know that name, Louis?" asked Saporta.

"Yes, and she's in the Vice Squad, like he said."

"You see: I'm not trying to put anything over on you," Krantz pointed out timidly.

"If I had a bow and arrow," said Paulo, "I'd shoot you. You're not worth a bullet."

"Roll up your sleeve," said Louis, preparing a hypodermic needle and a tourniquet.

"What's that?" asked Krantz, alarmed.

"Something to help you sleep."

"If I have to die, I'd rather be shot."

"Don't be scared of a little needle," said Saporta. "You'll wake up. Just remember one thing: whatever you do, I'll find out about it."

Krantz was somewhat reassured by these last words. He rolled up his sleeve and held out his arm to Louis. A few minutes later he fell asleep, for good. It was what Saporta called a heart attack.

"Are we going to visit that woman now?" asked Paulo.

"No," Saporta answered. "She's a cop. We have to take it easy. If she'd already put that tape in circulation, I'd know about it. We've got time. Be patient."

Gorodish liked to get up early. At eight-fifteen he was back home with a pile of newspapers. The apartment was beginning to be comfortable. It had a big leather sofa, some low, deep armchairs, and a reclining chair that was ideal for reading or listening to music.

He put the newspapers on the glass-topped table and went out onto the terrace that surrounded the apartment. Big glass doors opened onto it from the bedrooms. He stopped a moment to look at Alba nestled in her down-filled sleeping bag. When she was asleep, her calm, slightly sulky face and long blond hair made her look like a young goddess at rest. Gorodish couldn't help smiling. He knew his life was going to be full of surprises.

He made breakfast: black coffee for himself, cold banana Nesquik for Alba, toast, butter, and jam. He put it all on the table, then went into Alba's room and woke her with a kiss on the forehead. She grumbled and slid down farther into her sleeping bag.

Ten minutes later she came in wearing a black wool leotard.

"You've already walked across Paris and back?"

"Almost. I went to get the papers."

"You're going to read all that?"

"Yes, and so are you."

"What for?"

"You'll see. There are all kinds of things in the newspapers, things that may be useful to us. With a little practice, you'll learn to pick out the right articles."

"Will you tell me which ones they are?" she asked with a winsome smile.

"No. You'll have to learn to recognize them on your own."

"Oh, all right."

Alba concentrated on her breakfast. After eating several pieces of toast and jam, she lay down on the sofa and assumed a languid pose worthy of a Hollywood star.

"Do you like your new stereo?"

"Yes, it's very good. And so is the record you gave me. How do you know about Jorge Bolet?"

"Instinct. You'll have another one later today."

"You're planning to steal it?"

"No, somebody's giving it to me. I met him yesterday. He's a messenger for RCA, young and very nice. I'm having lunch with him today. He'll be a good connection, right?"

"Maybe," Gorodish said indifferently.

"Shall we listen to your record?"

He put it on the stereo. They listened in silence. Alba was beginning to like that kind of music. Afterward, they spent two hours going through the newspapers. He asked questions to find out what she had noticed. Her ideas were a little confused, but she would improve with practice.

Alba had hoped he would show a touch of jealousy when she told him about her lunch date with Jules, but the old fox hadn't taken the bait.

Paula woke up late. Her alarm clock hadn't gone off. Before doing anything else, she made sure the cassette was still there. She left half an hour later.

As soon as she was outside, she spotted a big Mercedes and three men who seemed to be waiting. Something tightened in her stomach and a quiver ran through her body. She started off along the sidewalk on the same side of the street as the Mercedes. She didn't have to look back. She heard a car door close. She was being followed.

She walked another hundred feet, trying to act as if she hadn't noticed anything, then hailed a taxi coming from Les Invalides.

"Place de l'Etoile," she told the driver.

"Let me off at the Quick-Elysée," said Paula.

She sat down at one of the outside tables and ordered a cup of coffee. She didn't see the Mercedes, but a few minutes later two of the men came in and went to the bar.

Paula was afraid. The cassette was in the pocket of her raincoat. She resisted an urge to touch it. She could try to slip away from them in one of the shopping galleries on the Champs-Elysées, but that might force them into action. She wondered why they hadn't tried to take the cassette from her on the stairs of her building.

A dozen contradictory plans flashed into her mind. She finally decided she would try to put the cassette in a safe place, then pretend to take a casual stroll and come back for it as soon as she managed to slip away from the men following her. The problem was to find a safe hiding place for the cassette. She thought of going downstairs to the bathroom, but she was sure she'd be followed there, and that might be dangerous.

She paid for her coffee and began slowly walking along the Champs-Elysées, making no effort to get away from the men following her. She desperately looked around for a place where she could furtively put the cassette, but she saw nothing that didn't seem too risky.

Jules had been riding all over Paris since nine o'clock, constantly looking at his watch, waiting for the fateful hour.

At five minutes to ten he leaned his motorbike against a tree in front of RCA and went to the nearest phone booth. After waiting a minute or two, he heard the warm, melodious voice of his Diva.

"Good morning, this is Jules."

"Do you still like the gown?"

"Yes, of course. . . ."

"I was thinking of inviting you to lunch but it's impossible. I've got a lot of appointments and I have to work with Geoffrey, my pianist, because he's about to go to Cologne. But you can call me again tomorrow morning if you want to. I may have more time then."

"We'll have lunch together?"

"Maybe."

"I keep thinking about your concert . . ."

"It's nice of you to say so."

"All right, I'll call you tomorrow."

"Good-bye."

Jules could hardly believe what he had just heard. Important people had been waiting for days to see Cynthia Hawkins, and she was going to slip him in ahead of them. He went up to the RCA offices. He had a huge bundle of records to pick up because he wanted to group all his afternoon deliveries so he could spend more time with Alba. Among other things, he had to go to the main studios of French national television, at Les Buttes-Chaumont, to supply the bigwigs with the latest releases.

Paula passed Le Drugstore, turned into the Avenue Matignon and decided to go on trying to find a hiding place for the cassette. As she walked, she took it out of her pocket and slipped it into the sleeve of her raincoat.

A mirror showed her that the men were about a hundred feet behind her. A little ahead of her was a motorbike with one of its saddlebags open. She suddenly knew it was time to act. She didn't think about the risk. She lowered her arm and felt the cassette slide into her hand. Then, just when her hand was above the saddlebag, she dropped the cassette, without slowing down. She heard it fall. Her heart was pounding. She could only hope the men hadn't noticed what she had done.

She heard heavy tires on the slope of the sidewalk, moving toward the parking places, and realized it was Saporta's Mercedes.

The massive, silent front of the car pulled up beside her. A riot-police van was parked less than fifty yards away. The Mercedes passed her. She recognized Saporta in the backseat. The third man was probably following on foot. The driver stopped and backed up to park. Saporta got out. He came toward her, smiling, looking like a courteous businessman. From the photographs she had seen of him, she would have imagined him as more brutal, less urbane.

"I believe you know who I am. I'd like to have a talk with you. May I invite you to get into my car?"

Paula was startled. It was hard to believe he

intended to kidnap her in front of a van full of policemen armed with submachine guns. She no longer had the cassette and she wasn't in danger. Saporta wasn't the type who would shoot a police inspector.

"Will it take long?"

"Only a few minutes, at most."

He opened the door for her. She sat in the middle of the backseat. While Saporta was sitting down beside her, Paulo opened the other door and got in. She was guarded on both sides.

"You know what I want, don't you?" Saporta asked almost timidly.

"A cassette, I suppose."

"You've guessed it."

"I'm surprised that a man like you waited so long to come to me."

"You mean you don't have the cassette on you?"

"Sorry to disappoint you, but it's already in the proper hands."

"Would you mind telling me how it got there?"

"At first I was going to keep it till this morning but I changed my mind during the night. I had a motorcycle policeman come and get it. I was afraid you might pay me a visit."

"Why were you afraid? As you can see, I have no intention of harming you. May I ask you what time the policeman came for the cassette?"

Paula hesitated a second. She sensed that there was some sort of trap in his question.

"A little after midnight."

Her hunch was right. Saporta clenched his teeth.

"Are you sure you don't have it on you?" he asked a little brusquely.

"Do you want to search me?"

"Why not? With your permission, of course."

Paulo's expert hands moved over her from her shoulders to her boots.

"Small caliber," he remarked, feeling her pistol.

"It's not the size of the gun that matters, it's how you use it. I don't have to tell you that. Are you satisfied?"

"She hasn't got it," Paulo informed his boss.

Saporta was a little pale. He didn't answer immediately, but he quickly regained his self-assurance.

"Thank you for being so cooperative. May I take you somewhere?"

"I appreciate the offer, but I'm going to a place where people wouldn't understand very well why I had the honor of your company."

"As you like."

Saporta got out and held the door for her. She began walking in the same direction as before, breathing deeply. The air had a faint smell of autumn and dead leaves.

The Mercedes left its parking place, passed her and disappeared on the Avenue Matignon. Not ruling out the possibility that Paulo might come back on foot, she stopped beside the police van, showed her card, and asked to have a few temporary bodyguards. The captain accompanied her personally, with two of his machine-gun-carrying men.

Paula walked back in the other direction. Suddenly she had the horrible feeling that the earth had opened up beneath her: the motorbike was gone.

Jean Saporta dialed a number. A man at Vice Squad headquarters answered.

"This is Jean."

"A problem?" asked the policeman.

"We're in trouble up to our ears. A very dangerous cassette was turned over to the police last night."

"Who's it from?"

"One of my people, by way of Paula Dumézil. She says a motorcycle cop picked it up at her apartment last night."

"It didn't come here. I'd have heard about it."

"Maybe it's at Narcotics."

"I'll find out. Call me back in an hour."

Wearing skintight jeans, a bulky blue sweater, and new boots, Alba had been waiting in front of Lido-Musique for several minutes when she saw Jules arrive on his motorbike. He looked as if he had just had a divine revelation.

"Where do you want to go?" he asked.

"Le Drugstore."

"Okay, I'll leave my bike here and my packages in the Lido."

They went up the Champs-Elysées. Jules walked sideways so he could have a better look at the young goddess who had suddenly dropped into his life. He handed her the record he had brought for her, a Horowitz Chopin album.

"Here. It's fantastic, you'll see."

"Thanks very much. You're so nice you deserve a kiss," she said, going into action before she had time to see that he was blushing.

They found a corner table and sat down facing each other. Jules took off his jacket while Alba looked over the menu.

"I want a hamburger special."

"Me too. What do you want to drink?"

"Apple juice."

When they had ordered, they looked at each other in silence for a long time, engrossed in their mutual discovery.

"I'd like to ride around Paris with you on your motorbike," she said. "I don't know the city very well yet. I came here only a few days ago."

"Where are you from?"

"A little town in the middle of nowhere."

"During the day, the cops would stop me if I let you ride on my bike with me."

"Then we'll go out at night, or else I'll steal a motorbike for myself."

"You can go out at night?"

"I do as I please. You too?"

"Yes. I live alone and make my own living. I'm free. You don't live with your parents?"

"No."

"You rent a room?"

"No, I have a sort of stepfather. His name is Serge and he's wonderful. He took me away from my little town because he thinks I'm gifted. He takes care of me."

"Good, we can go to movies together, or do other things."

"Serge doesn't even want to put me in high school. He says the teachers are too stupid. He's going to find some smart people to come and teach me at home. But he hasn't started looking for anybody yet, so I'm free all day. If you want to, you can stop by and see me when you're making your deliveries. I'll give you my address and phone number."

"I often have spare time. Do you have a good stereo at home?"

"Yes, a terrific one. Serge just bought it. He's crazy about classical music. I'm learning about it from him. Before, I was mainly into singers like Patti Smith. Excuse me a minute, I'll be right back."

"Sure."

He watched her walk away. What luck, meeting a girl like her! When she talked to him, he felt as if she were looking right through him, and there was always a mysterious smile behind her eyes.

The waiter brought the food. Alba came back a minute later. She sat down, lifted her sweater, and took out a book, giving Jules a glimpse of her smooth, white belly.

"Here, it's a present."

"A book about Maria Callas!"

"I stole it for you. Nobody saw me. Do you like it?"

"I sure do!"

"Then kiss me. That's what you're supposed to do when somebody gives you a present."

They leaned forward over their hamburgers and their cool cheeks touched each other.

"Would you like to go to the opera with me some night?"

"I'd like it very much," said Alba, smothering her French fries in ketchup.

"I've got hundreds of records and tapes at home. You'll have to come there."

"Is that all you think about?"

"Is what all I think about?"

"Music."

"Not really. . . . Can you come tomorrow night?"

"Where do you live?"

"Far away, in the Twentieth Arrondissement, on the outer boulevards."

"All right, I'll take the subway."
Jules began reciting:

> "Nel profondo
> Cieco mondo
> si precipiti la sorte
> Già spietata a questo cor.
> Vincerà l'amor più forte
> con l'aita del valor."

"Is that an Italian poem?" asked Alba.
"It's what Marilyn Horne sings in Vivaldi's *Orlando Furioso*."
"Isn't he the one who composed *The Four Seasons*?" she said, frowning.
"Exactly."
"You see? I do know a little bit about music."

Fifty minutes after his first call, Saporta dialed the same number.
"This is Jean again."
"It looks like there's nothing to worry about," the policeman in the Vice Squad told him. "Everything's calm here. There's been no talk about you at all. I'll call you if I find out anything. Are you sure Paula had that cassette?"
"Absolutely."
"I'll do everything I can."
"You'd better, because the cassette is as dangerous for you as it is for me."
"They've never gotten us yet, have they?"

Ten minutes after Paula called him, Boulanger, the head of the Vice Squad, arrived on the scene, followed by a car full of inspectors. Paula got into the black Peugeot, deathly white, and told the whole story.

Boulanger flew into a rage. He took immediate measures, assigned various parts of the city to his inspectors and ordered them to stop all messengers on motorbikes. They had to get that cassette at any cost.

Jules listened to the superb recording of Mozart's *Don Giovanni* conducted by Carlo Maria Giulini, and then, after a half-hour pause while he floated in space, he again listened to the tape of his sublime Diva, holding her pearl-gray gown against his face. Her image filled his whole mind and body. He imagined her in his arms, he savored the taste of her kisses. Suddenly he had an idea. He connected his cassette recorder to his Nagra and made a copy of the first half of the concert.

At one in the morning he got on his motorbike and rode along the boulevards to the Place de l'Etoile. The night was clear and fragrant. It wasn't too cold. He dreamed of a body against his.

After turning into the Avenue Foch, he entered the narrower street that ran parallel to it, separated from it by a strip of grass and trees. Traffic was heavier here. Soon, in the glare of the headlights, he saw the first beautiful, sensual black women, sinuous as the night, wearing shorts or slit skirts that exposed their magic legs to the admiration of potential customers.

Jules slipped between the cars and slowly rode past the women, dazzled by their beauty, brimming over with joy, enchanted by a smile or the pose of a body.

He stopped in front of a tall woman who seemed

as lithe and smooth as a black panther. She had a short Afro, the kind he liked. He finished making up his mind when he looked at her delicate features, almond-shaped eyes and soft, voluptuous lips, open like an unknown fruit.

He parked his motorbike on the sidewalk. She took him by the hand and led him to her room.

"What's your name?"

"Karina. And yours?"

"Jules. I want to ask you something. . . . I'm madly in love with a black singer. I have one of her dresses under my jacket. Will you put it on and then take it off while we listen to her sing?"

He showed her his cassette player.

"I'm willing. I like customers who want harmless things like that. You'll give me a little extra, won't you?"

"Of course."

"I think we'll get along just fine with each other."

Karina lit a candle that gave off orangeish light. Like a sultan reclining on his cushions, Jules watched her play the part of a singer. The cassette was turning in his Sony. He was fascinated.

Karina took off the pearl-gray gown very slowly. It slid over her dark body like the skin of a snake. Half of Jules' body followed the modulations of the music, the other half responded to Karina's charms.

The gown dropped to the floor. Karina knelt between Jules' legs. He admired her uptilted breasts and the dark, rounded mass below her belly. He abandoned himself and lay back among the cushions. Her mouth made him forget the music. Soon she slid under him. He penetrated her gently. She smiled, amused by his pleasure, and pulled his chest down against her. The feel of her body, firm as ebony yet soft as a breeze, her hands gliding over his skin, the touch of her frizzy hair against his cheek, and finally her fingernails digging into his flesh—all this brought him to a peak of ecstasy.

Afterward, as they lay side by side, he smiled happily.

"I hope you'll come back," she said.

"I'd like to. Are you here every night?"

"Yes."

That night, Jules dreamed a lot.

CHAPTER FOUR

BOULANGER WAS MAKING AN ALL-OUT EFFORT. Since seven in the morning, inspectors and uniformed cops had been grabbing all the messengers who showed up in the streets, and searching their saddlebags.

Paula was one of the investigators who were trying to draw up a complete list of the messengers employed by companies that had their offices in buildings near the place where she had dropped off the precious cassette. There were some whose addresses could be found, and then there were the others, those who were paid for each delivery and had no salary. As soon as a partial list was drawn up, six inspectors began ringing doorbells, but they usually found no one home. Tension was rising.

What the police didn't know was that their operations were being closely followed by a dozen men who were far from being reputable citizens. Saporta had carefully chosen them. In a room in the Hôtel George-V, he was waiting beside the phone after having spent a rather agitated night. All the activities of his organization had been reduced to a minimum, all narcotics transfers had been suspended; in the underworld, everyone was either taking time off or keeping tabs on the hunt for the messenger.

At five minutes to nine, a motorbike left the Place de la Concorde and started up the Champs-Elysées. Even from a helicopter, anyone would have noticed the ecstatic way Jules zoomed in and out of traffic. This morning it was *Tosca*, sung by Leontyne Price, that lifted him into euphoria. His cassette player was solidly anchored in the cigar box behind the windshield, and he listened with ineffable delight to the soaring sounds of the singer's magnificent voice.

When he reached the Rond-Point des Champs-Elysées he turned right, into the Avenue Matignon. His eyes soon registered the subtle charm of police uniforms.

The cops, who had the word "messenger" engraved in the soft folds of their brains, all reacted at once. Jules' sensitive ears were assaulted by a strident symphony of whistles.

In his head, everything took on the jerky motion of an old silent film. Conjectures popped in and out of his mind with the speed of machine-gun bullets. Among them was the idea that his Diva had reported him to the police for stealing her gown.

The cops were converging on him, pointing to the exact spot on the pavement where he was supposed to stop.

Jules didn't know why all these cops were here, but one thing seemed clear to him: he mustn't stop. He avoided the first two with a sudden swerve and barely passed between the next pair. Seeing that he would have a hard time getting through the rest of the cops who were already clustering to block the Avenue Matignon, he swung left in a more or less controlled skid and took off down the Rue de Ponthieu at top speed.

The cops' Renault 12 made a rubber-burning start and a short run in the illegal direction of the one-way street, then turned in pursuit of Jules. The tachometer needle jumped into the red warning zone as the engine gave its all.

Ignoring traffic lights and right-of-way, Jules roared along at full throttle, but the cops' siren was coming closer and closer while Leontyne Price imperturbably continued her sublime performance.

Meanwhile other police cars were cruising on the Champs-Elysées in the hope of catching Jules at one of the cross streets.

The Renault was about to overtake him when a driver up ahead, blithely unaware of what was going on behind him, slowed down at the sight of a parking place. Jules turned abruptly, crashed into the curb, bounced onto the sidewalk, just missed the elegant lady who had stopped to look at a window display, and then he dashed back into the street while the cops were apopletically trying to explain that they had to get through. Jules quickly took a two-hundred-yard lead. He was beginning to rejoice when he saw a truck stopped in the middle of the street. The driver was delivering a case of bottles.

Strongly suspecting that more cops were waiting for him at the end of the street, Jules suddenly had the idea of going through the Galerie Point-Show, a shopping arcade which opened onto the Champs-Elysées.

His front wheel brutally flung open the glass

door, nearly flattening a shopper. He rode past stores, a restaurant, bewildered faces, a sandwich shop, a pharmacy, a movie house, and the Sony showroom. There, he stopped and got off his motorbike to check the lay of the land before making his exit. No cops on the horizon. He crossed the avenue, took the Rue Marbeuf and kept going till he reached the Left Bank, where he was reasonably sure there would be less interest in him.

It wasn't till he stopped at a café for a beer that he began trembling. That big swarm of cops would make sense if they were after someone who had just shot his way out of prison, but all Jules had done was to steal a dress and then bring it back. That hardly seemed like enough to throw the police into an uproar. There was something he didn't understand but he couldn't imagine what it might be. Maybe it wasn't even true that his Diva had turned him in. Would she really do such a thing?

Gorodish was calmly strolling along the Boulevard Saint-Germain. Now and then he stopped in front of a display window to admire a painted wooden buddha, a piece of furniture, or a picture.

He had seldom felt as good as he did now. He knew he would soon have to start thinking about setting up some kind of a job. He and Alba were spending money like crazy, but his bank account was still a long way from hitting bottom. He was concerned about the future because big jobs sometimes required heavy investment and not many bankers would give a loan to someone in his profession.

He arrived at Pan-Musique just as Mr. Milletre, the owner, was opening for the day's business. Since Gorodish couldn't get along with only five or six records, he went in and let himself go. He bought Gustav Mahler's ten symphonies, Richard Strauss's *Der Rosenkavalier* and *Don Quixote*, Schoenberg's quartets, an album of Schubert piano sonatas, Beethoven's nine symphonies conducted by Klemperer, Beethoven's quartets, trios, and piano sonatas, Béla Bartók's second violin concerto, Bach's Musical Offering and works for solo violin, and Mozart's quartets.

Mr. Milletre kept his usual calm. The day was off to a good start. He gave Gorodish a twenty-percent discount.

Gorodish patiently made five trips to carry all the records to his apartment, where his little angel, lying on the carpet, was conscientiously going through the morning papers. She was casually dressed in a black satin garter belt with matching panties and stockings. Comfortably ensconced among her cushions, she dunked a piece of toast in a cup of hot chocolate while she turned the pages.

Gorodish put Mahler's Sixth on the stereo. It would take at least that to soothe him after the excitement of buying all those records. He sat down in his reclining chair, put his feet up and tried to listen while he looked at Alba. He felt as if his body were dissolving into the strings of the orchestra. What an inspired composer that Mahler was!

Jules was beginning to recover. To set things straight in his mind, he decided to call his Diva.

"Ah, it's you, Jules. I'm just waking up," replied a foggy voice.

"*I'm* wide awake, believe me. What I've been through this morning is enough to keep me awake for days. It was a real manhunt. The cops came after me like a bunch of mad hornets. I don't know what came over me but instead of stopping I speeded up, and I managed to get away from them. I was afraid because of your gown. You didn't tell them I took it, did you?"

"If you think I did that, there's no use coming to see me," said Cynthia, offended.

"I was in such a panic I didn't know what to think. Even so, it didn't seem to me that all those cops would be after me just for stealing a dress."

"Now you're talking more sensibly."

"Why could they have wanted me?"

"Maybe there was a robbery and they thought you were someone else. Or maybe it was only for a routine check, how should I know? You should have stopped."

"That's true. But when it happened, I had a bad feeling . . ."

"Don't think about it anymore. You're safe now."

"I'd like to see you when I finish my work."

"What time?"

"About six o'clock."

"Okay, I'll see you then, you gangster."

Simon Weinstadt looked happy. Cynthia rejoined him, more resplendent than ever.

"I told you we'd have a lot of offers in Europe after your first concert," he said. "Here are the ones that have come in so far. Abbado wants you to do *Salome* at La Scala in 1986. Karajan would like a recital for the Salzburg Festival in 1985, and he hopes to find a closer date for an orchestral concert in Berlin; we haven't yet discussed the program. Alfredo Katz is also very enthusiastic. He'd like *Tosca* with James Levine in 1985. Covent Garden would like *Lulu* with Boulez. Muti suggests Strauss's *Four Last Songs*, immediately after your London recital. Jessye Norman is ill. Then there are some less important things."

"That's a good beginning."

"There are also other offers that are . . . a bit thorny, but very interesting. . . ."

"You're talking about record companies, aren't you?"

"Exactly. The DGG people came here from Hamburg specially for the concert. They're willing to do anything to get you, and because of Karajan's commitments they have some specific plans to offer you. Decca came from London, Philips from Amsterdam, and even the Japanese are here, not to mention EMI, RCA, and a French company, Erato. They're all ready to sign an exclusive contract, with a recording program spread over several years."

"Look, Simon, record companies have been offering me contracts like that for years. Since I didn't accept them in New York, why should I accept them here? You know what I think of records. I can't work miracles without an audience."

"Concerts can be recorded live, you know. I've looked into that possibility . . ."

"No recording can ever measure up to my standards of how a voice should sound. But even if that were possible, I'd still be appalled at the idea that a moment of magic could be reproduced tens of thousands of times. That's not art. And there are always little imperfections that are acceptable only because they're unique; I wouldn't want them to be recorded and played over and over."

"What if you'd agreed to a recording of your concert the other night? Everything was sublime."

"Maybe for the first time in my career."

"Well, then?"

"It doesn't change anything, as far as I'm concerned. The people who were at the concert will remember it."

"But for the complete development of your career, records are..."

"Glenn Gould made records and didn't give any concerts. With me, it's the opposite, and there's nothing more to be said."

"All right, I won't argue. But for the sake of music, I hope you change your mind someday."

Nadia had a fever and she was shivering. She no longer knew if it was day or night. She slept sporadically and woke up in the middle of nightmares, with fear in her belly. She was hungry and thirsty; no one had brought her anything since the time when she was locked up.

She would have given anything for a blanket, water, and bread. She knew Saporta was capable of letting her die there, without lifting a finger to help her in any way. She didn't even have the strength to scream.

Jules had just spent an hour with Cynthia. They had talked about music. She had asked him questions about the way he lived, but he hadn't had much to say about it because his life was taken up almost entirely with music.

He left the Ritz and got back on his flying carpet. He didn't see the two Japanese from Nippon Columbia waiting for him inside their Toyota.

He looked at his watch. Alba was supposed to come at eight o'clock. He just had time to do some shopping.

Since his notions of culinary art were rather skimpy, he bought a roasted chicken, potato chips, a salad, cottage cheese in cardboard containers, cans of beer and coke, and two pounds of fresh dates.

Since his Diva had assured him that he was in no danger, his mind was at peace as he climbed the stairs to his apartment.

The Japanese parked their Toyota near his building. Sitting behind its tinted glass, they wondered if they were on the right track; but since, in their well-organized heads, no normal, innocuous explanation could justify meetings between Cynthia Hawkins and a messenger from RCA, they decided to wait.

Alba was a little late because she had taken time to get a pair of fur-lined gloves for Jules. She liked to give presents. To find something to go with the gloves, she had rummaged through her stock of stolen objects and chosen a beautiful Omega wristwatch made of shiny steel.

Jules was tasting his salad dressing, and noting that it had a litle too much vinegar, when Alba knocked on the door.

She kissed him, standing on tiptoe (he was six feet one), and handed him the gloves. He thanked her for them.

"I like your place," she said. "We live the same way, on the floor. Chairs, tables, beds, and all that stuff are a waste of money. Do you mind if I look around?"

"Go ahead, look at anything you want."

Alba was impressed by the number of records and tapes that filled the shelves.

"This is all classical music?"

"I also have some Indian, Arab, and Japanese music."

"Serge went on a shopping spree today. He came back with at least fifty records, maybe more. He's like you; he's all wrapped up in music. Not that I have anything against it, you understand. I like it, in fact, and before long I'll know more about it. There's a lot to learn. Those composers didn't waste their time, you can see that from all the records there are in stores." She stopped in front of the photographs of singers. "Who are all these women? I hope you're not one of those men who collect pictures of all the women they've gone to bed with."

"They're singers."

"Oh . . . Do you paint?"

"No, but a painter lived here before I did. He's the one who made those spots on the floor. Are you hungry?"

"I'm starving."

"I bought a few things. Come."

He had put the food on the floor in front of the mattress. Alba was at ease. She looked at a pile of new records that he hadn't yet put away.

"I'd like you to play something beautiful while we eat."

Jules hesitated, then put on a record of selections of Puccini operas sung by Maria Callas. It was a good choice for openers.

He sat down beside Alba, clumsily cut up the chicken and realized that he had forgotten to buy bread. She watched him, amused. He opened a can of Coke for her, after she had refused a beer. Then he reached into his clothes cabinet, took out a red cotton scarf and spread it over the lamp to dim the light.

"That's better," said Alba.

As they listened to Maria Callas, they enthusiastically dug into the potato chips, and the still-warm chicken lost its legs and wings. Alba ate everything with her fingers, even the salad. Jules washed away the cares of the day with several cans of Carlsberg.

One of the Japanese had left the car to buy sandwiches in a nearby café. It was a scanty meal for them, without raw fish or sake, but Kazuhichi Tsukahara was determined to let nothing stop him from getting Cynthia Hawkins to sign a contract.

When the cottage cheese containers were empty, nothing was left but the dates. Alba and Jules quickly finished them off. She changed her mind about the beer and drank a can of it. Then she stretched out her legs, settled herself comfortably among the cushions and decided it was time to give Jules the watch.

"Come here," she said. "Hold out your left hand." She unbuckled his cheap, battered wristwatch and took the Omega from the pocket of her jeans. "This means a lot to me because it's one of the first things I ever stole, but now I want you to have it."

Since Jules was getting used to his recent successes with women, he kissed her before she could ask him to.

"I want to play something wonderful for you, a tape I recorded. A pirate tape. That's my specialty. All these tapes were recorded during concerts. I have a whole setup for it."

"What kind of setup?"

"All my equipment is hidden in that violin case over there in the corner."

"Not bad."

"This is my latest tape; I just made it. A fantastic black American singer."

"Cynthia Hawkins?"

"You know Cynthia Hawkins?"

"I know about her."

Jules was a bit taken aback. He connected the headsets to the amplifier, adjusted them, and put one of them over Alba's ears, after pushing her blond hair out of the way. She was docile, ready to let herself be carried away by the music.

She heard the silence, then the piano, then the voice. Jules was beside her, also wearing headphones, and they held hands.

Alba felt something liquefying in her body. New sensations ran through her. The voice gently took her further and further, deeper and deeper. She was almost afraid. She was entering an unknown realm. Her whole body let itself go. As though to assure herself that she wasn't making the journey alone, she moved closer to Jules. He took her in his arms.

When the tape ended, they took off their headsets and remained in each other's arms a long time, exchanging kisses that would have left a long-distance runner breathless.

At three in the morning, Alba thought it might be time for her to go home. Jules gave her duplicate keys to his apartment, so she could come there whenever she wanted, and called for a taxi. They went downstairs together, without speaking.

Jules waited till the taxi had disappeared, then went back upstairs. He had always thought there were divinities who presided over musical matters, and this time he felt their radiance warming his soul and body.

Tenacious as always, the Japanese followed the taxi and carefully noted the blond girl's address before going back to their rooms at the Hôtel Nikko.

* * *

Gorodish heard the elevator and took a deep breath.

Alba was frightened by the sound of the bell that dinged each time the elevator came to a different floor of the building. Something told her she might have gone a little too far. I hope he's asleep, she thought.

When she went into the living room and saw Serge there, her legs became wobbly and she felt as if his eyes were going to pin her to the wall, like a rare butterfly.

"If you pull one more stunt like this, I'll take you back to your mangy town and you can while away the time cooking for your father and wiping your little brother's ass."

"I'm sorry, I won't do it again."

"We won't talk about it anymore. It's settled."

Gorodish's face changed. Alba let the air out of her lungs. She had understood.

"Shall I make us some Nesquik?" she suggested.

"Okay."

She went into the kitchen and stayed there till she got a grip on herself. When she came back with the glasses of Nesquik she sat down beside Gorodish on the sofa. He realized that since she had resisted her inclination to sit on the floor, his threat to take her back to her hometown had shaken her and she was trying to please him.

"Jules played something fantastic for me tonight."

"Rock?"

"No, an American singer, Cynthia Hawkins."

"A record?" Gorodish asked shrewdly.

"No, a tape."

"Ah . . ."

"Music never made me feel that way before. It

was wonderful, like I was flying. . . ."

"Where did he get that tape?"

"He made it himself, at a concert. That's his specialty. He hides his equipment in a violin case."

"A cassette recorder?"

"No, some kind of super, extraspecial tape recorder. A Magra, or something like that."

"Aside from the piano and the singer's voice, what else did you hear on the tape?"

"Applause, sometimes a cough."

"No noise from the tape itself?"

"No, I don't think so."

Gorodish smiled broadly. He seemed happy about something.

"You've been reading the papers, haven't you?"

"Of course. In fact, that's why I recognized Cynthia Hawkins' name when Jules said it to me."

"You see? Reading the papers can be useful. What else do you remember about Cynthia Hawkins, besides her name?"

"She's a star in America, this was her first concert in Europe, everyone thought it was terrific. That's all."

"You're forgetting the most important thing."

"What's that?"

"Cynthia Hawkins has never appeared on radio or television, she's never made a record, there's no recording of her voice in existence, and her concert the other night may have been the best one of her life."

"That's right, I remember now."

"Are you beginning to understand?"

"Yes. I think it's a super idea."

"Now I'm very glad you went out tonight."

"I bet we'll make a big pile of money from this. But we won't cheat Jules, will we?"

"No, he'll get his share. As soon as you wake up tomorrow morning, call him and invite him to dinner. Does he have a phone?"

"Yes."

Serge and Alba finished their Nesquik and went to bed. She would have liked to stay with him but she had a feeling it would be better not to push things tonight, so she slipped into her down-filled bag and drifted off to sleep, thinking of Jules' kisses and Serge's face.

CHAPTER FIVE

I T WAS PAST NINE O'CLOCK WHEN JULES WOKE up. Since he didn't want to run into the cops again, he decided to call RCA and say he was sick. A case of the flu would do the job.

"Hello, Myriam, this is Jules."

"I was wondering what became of you. Everyone's in a panic here. There are cops all over the place. Some inspectors came to ask for the addresses of the messengers."

"Did you give them mine?"

"I had to. What's the matter, have you done something?"

"No. Except that when some cops blew their whistles at me yesterday I got scared and kept going."

"They're stopping all messengers. I don't know why, but it seems to be something serious."

"I called to say I've got the flu. Will you fix things up for me?"

"Sure, don't worry. I'll talk to the personnel manager."

"Thanks. If you find out anything, please call me."

"I will. I'll keep checking on the manhunt. So long."

Jules was surprised that the police hadn't already come to his apartment. But after all, he wasn't the only messenger in Paris. Even so, he decided it would be better not to hang around much longer. Since he had run away from the cops, they wouldn't just let him go if they got their hands on him.

Ten minutes later, wearing his gloves, he rode off on his motorbike after putting the latest Leontyne Price recording, a Schumann recital, on his cassette player. The sky was clear. A cool little breeze played with his face.

Karina was as beautiful in daylight as she was at night. It was three-thirty in the afternoon. She had been lounging around her apartment, listening to disco and polishing her nails.

The doorbell rang. It was her pimp, stopping by to take sixty percent of her earnings from the night before. He was called Jeff. Like all members of Saporta's network, he was dressed with discreet elegance. No patent-leather shoes or pink Cadillacs for Saporta's men. He wanted them to look neutral. A neutrality lightly perfumed with money, nothing more.

Jeff never said anything till after his share of the receipts had been handed over to him. Today, since the amount was bigger than usual, he sat down on a corner of the bed to talk awhile.

"Is everything all right?"

"No problems," said Karina. "The customers aren't too hard to get along with these days. They start getting worked up in spring, and now they're okay. . . . It's been a long time since we spent a weekend together."

"I know, but I'm very busy right now."

"You've got a lot of business?"

"No, business is the same as usual, but the boss wants to get hold of some stupid little messenger who keeps giving us the slip."

"It's funny you should say that, because I had a messenger the other night. He was nice."

"Tell me about him."

"He was young, eighteen or twenty. He had a long dress with him, and he had me put it on and pretend to be an opera singer."

"Do you know who he works for?"

"A record company. I think he said it was RCA."

At these words, Jeff's heart began pounding like a jackhammer.

"My God! That was our messenger! And we missed a chance to get him! Did you treat him right?"

"Yes. He said he'd come back, but you know how it is, they all say that."

"I'll give you a phone number. Call it right away if he does come back. It'll be good for you and me both. I'll take you to Deauville."

"For a whole weekend?"

"Three days, if you want. Pass the word to the other girls, in case he decides to try somebody else. Now you see why I keep telling you to do a good job with your customers so they'll want to come back for more."

Paula had just checked her sixth messenger. Since she hadn't yet taken time for lunch, she stopped at a café not far from Jules' address. He was next on her list.

After a ham and cheese sandwich and a glass of

Beaujolais, she went to Jules' apartment. No answer to her knock. She took out her passkeys and opened the door. She had a search warrant for each address.

Her eyes opened wide when she saw the row of cassettes.

She began doing her work with painstaking care. The cassette she was looking for was a Memorex C-60, but she saw only Agfa or BASF cassettes. She couldn't fail to notice how much Jules seemed to like opera. At last a Memorex. Paula nervously took it out. The inscription she read on the label shot down her hope: UN BALLO IN MASCHERA/PRICE. She admired the stereo. Not bad for a messenger. It must have taken all his money, because there was hardly any furniture in the place. She searched in the pockets of his clothes, under the mattress, and everywhere else. Suddenly she realized she had forgotten to check the cassette player of the stereo. It was empty.

Jules looked at his new Omega every few minutes. It was a superb watch. He was proud that it had been stolen by Alba. To pass the time, he decided to call her. Maybe he could see her.

"Hello, this is Jules."

"You must have read my mind. I tried to call you a little while ago but there was no answer. I told Serge about your tape. He'd love to hear it. He wants you to come to dinner tonight."

"All right, but there's a problem: I can't go back to my apartment to get the tape. I'll explain when I see you."

"I can go and get it if you want me to."

"That's a good idea. Be sure not to lose the tape."

"Don't worry."

"What time shall I come for dinner?"

"Whenever you like, as soon as you're free. We're on the top floor."

"Okay, see you tonight."

Since Jules had nothing special to do, he decided to see a film. Pasolini's *Medea*, with Maria Callas, was being shown at a movie house in the Latin Quarter.

Hearing footsteps on the stairs, Paula sat down on the bed. Alba opened the door and wondered what the woman was doing there. Jules evidently wasn't stingy with his keys.

"Hello," Alba said coldly.

"Hello. I'm a friend of Jules'. Do you know if he'll be back soon?"

"I have no idea. He usually comes home about seven o'clock. You can wait for him."

"I will."

Ignoring Paula's presence, Alba opened the Nagra, took out the tape of the concert, and put it in its box.

"Good-bye," she said, scarcely looking at Paula.

She wondered why that woman hadn't taken off her raincoat. There was something stiff and formal about her. Maybe Jules liked mature women, as they were called in magazines.

Mohammed was waiting in his taxi. He took Alba home.

Gorodish didn't have the patience to wait for Jules. As soon as Alba came back, he put the tape on his Revox and settled into his reclining chair while she ran a bath for herself.

Technically, the tape was flawless. Musically, it

made Gorodish feel as if two big wings were carrying him through space. He had never heard anything like it.

When it ended, he carefully rewound it and put it back in its box. Then he went into the bathroom, where Alba's face and shoulders were floating above a thick layer of lavender-scented foam.

"How did you like the tape?"

"It's incredibly good. We'll be able to have the bathroom done over. You'll have your round Hollywood tub."

"We can take baths together in it. Are we going to a restaurant with Jules tonight?"

"No, we'll stay here. It'll be better for talking."

"There's nothing to eat here."

"I'll call a caterer."

Gorodish went back to the living room. He liked to see Alba with her hair pinned up, exposing the perfection of her neck. He wondered how she would be dressed that evening.

He called Chez Gargantua and ordered smoked salmon, roast beef, a vegetable puree, and a chocolate cake for Alba, plum and whisky sherbet for himself, champagne, and three bottles of Savigny-sur-Beaune.

When Jules arrived, the first thing he saw was Gorodish's face, which was always startling for someone not used to it. Then Alba appeared, draped in a big, white, silver-spangled scarf that enveloped her body like a fog, transparent enough to show the outlines of her delightful flesh and loose enough to reveal uncovered portions of it when she moved.

They listened to the tape. By the time the Diva had let the last note softly fade away, something important had happened among Serge, Alba, and Jules. The music had created a bond among them better than any words could have done and, in the silence, each of them was aware of it.

Just then the food was delivered. Since there was still no dining-room table, the three of them sat down on cushions around the low, glass-topped table in the living room. The waiter who came with the catered meal began serving it to them and kept the rest of it hot or cold, according to what was required, in the kitchen.

"By the way," Alba said casually to Jules, "there's a woman waiting for you in your apartment."

"What are you talking about?"

"I'm talking about the woman who was sitting on your bed when I came in. I wondered what she was doing there because she hadn't taken off her raincoat."

"Did you ask her what her name was?"

"No. I just took the tape. She asked me when you'd be back. I said I didn't know."

"No one else but you has a key to my apartment. How could she..."

"All I can tell you is that she was there."

"I can only think of two explanations: either she came to rob me, or she's a cop."

"Have you committed a crime?" asked Gorodish, smiling.

"Not really, but yesterday morning when I was riding on the Avenue Matignon, a bunch of cops blew their whistles at me and I didn't stop. They chased me awhile, then I got away from them."

"Why didn't you stop?"

Jules laughed.

"I was worried about what I did after Cynthia Hawkins' concert, when I went to her dressing room. I don't know why, but I stole the dress she'd worn for the concert."

"Ah, so you're the mysterious man I read about in *France-Soir*."

"Yes, but the papers didn't say what happened the next day. I felt bad about taking her dress, so I went to see her at the Ritz and gave it back to her."

Gorodish was becoming more and more interested.

"She didn't call the cops?" he asked.

"No. She was very nice. We had tea and then she gave me one of her other dresses."

"Have you seen her again?"

"Yes, almost every day."

"Does she know about the tape?"

"No. I'm afraid to tell her."

Gorodish emptied his glass. The champagne was a little too cold. The salmon, however, melted in his mouth.

"I want to offer you a chance to make some money, Jules."

"Now's a good time for it. I'd like to buy another Nagra."

"That tape is very valuable. If you're willing, I can handle the business of selling it. No one will know where it came from. The record companies have a lot of money. According to the papers, they're all trying to get a contract with Cynthia Hawkins. If they start bidding against each other, the price will rise fast and far."

"They've all got some of their people at the Ritz, waiting and hoping. And trying to get on the right side of Weinstadt."

"Who's that?"

"Cynthia's impresario in Europe. He has a lot of connections."

"Then he's the one to approach about the tape. The record companies will get wind of it."

"I've heard he's not easy to get along with. When one of his artists signs with a record company, he takes over the recording session in person and supervises everything. He's got a terrific ear."

"We'll let him hear the tape. As far as I can tell, it's perfect."

"I think so too."

"Are you willing to let me negotiate the sale?"

"Yes. How do you want to split the money?"

"Fifty-fifty."

"That's okay with me. How much can we ask?"

"We won't ask for anything. We'll auction off the tape to the highest bidder and the price will go up very fast."

"That's a good idea."

Alba took a sip of champagne, feeling important. After all, it was because of her that Serge and Jules had met.

Serge cut thin slices of roast beef. The waiter served the wine, wondering what could have brought that strange threesome together.

Paula was losing patience. Jules was probably in hiding. The longer she stayed in his apartment, the more clearly her intuition told her that she had found the right man. She decided to leave and come back the next morning, early enough to catch him while he was still in bed, unless he stayed away all night.

She left the apartment, locked the door, and went downstairs. As she was coming out of the building, she saw a blue Toyota with tinted glass pulling into the parking space. She continued on her way. Then, when the two Japanese got out of their car and walked toward Jules' building, she followed them, just in case.

Knowing that Jules was having dinner on the Rue de l'Université, the tenacious men from Nippon Columbia had decided to have a look at his apartment. Since they were neither cops nor robbers, it took them some time to get the door open. Paula, on the floor below, was amused by their efforts. She almost felt like lending them her passkey.

Finally the Japanese managed to get inside. As soon as they had closed the door behind them, they were overjoyed. All those records, all those pictures of singers, the expensive stereo—everything seemed to confirm their suspicions. Tsukahara stepped over to the violin case, a beautiful Hill case for two violins. He opened it and was so astounded at the sight of the Nagra that he cried out like a samurai drawing his sword.

It was all remarkably put together, with the microphones well positioned. When Tsukahara looked at the titles of the recordings, it was easy for him to understand why that messenger was on such good terms with Cynthia Hawkins.

There had to be a recording of her concert. The two men spent an hour searching the apartment from top to bottom, without finding the tape.

They were afraid of only one thing: that Jules had already sold the tape to RCA. But since they knew Weinstadt's reputation, they believed they would have been informed of it if it had happened. News traveled fast in the record business.

It was possible that they had a head start on their

competitors. To get that tape, they were determined
to stop at nothing.

Paula followed them to the Hôtel Nikko, then
she called headquarters and asked to have them kept
under surveillance. Maybe they were the connection
that would lead her to Jules.

After dinner, Jules went to another room for a
few moments to call his Diva. Without saying why
he wanted to see her, he asked if he could visit her
late that night, and she consented.

At one in the morning he left Gorodish and Alba,
ecstatic about his evening. He decided to leave his
motorbike in the neighborhood and go to the Ritz
in a taxi, to avoid attracting attention.

He padlocked his motorbike in front of the Li-
brairie La Hune, on the Boulevard Saint-Germain,
and took a taxi. As he was approaching the entrance
of the Ritz, he was surprised to realize how much
he trusted Gorodish, since he had let him keep the
tape of his Diva's concert.

JULES CROSSED THE LONG GALLERY WHERE two hundred display windows exhibited some of the most expensive merchandise in Paris. He walked between the big marble pillars, turned left, and went up the broad staircase leading to Cynthia's suite. He knocked on the door to the drawing room. Cynthia opened it, wearing a loose, sky-blue negligee. He stepped inside.

"What's going on, Jules?"

"I don't know," he said, taking off his jacket, "but I'm afraid."

They sat down on the sofa, facing the fireplace above which hung a tall nineteenth-century mirror that reflected their images. A big clock, candlesticks, and a bouquet of red gladiolus gave the room a look that was both colorful and subdued, and the silence that hung over it was like a finishing touch of luxury. Cynthia was beautiful. In the gentle light, her face had an almost coppery tinge.

"What are you afraid of?"

"Strange things have been happening the last few days. The police are looking for me and I don't know why. Someone came to search my apartment. I sometimes think I'm being followed. I have the feeling a lot of things are going on around me but I can't say exactly what they are."

"Why did you run away if you hadn't done anything wrong?"

"I don't know, I just did. But now I'm really starting to get scared."

"What can I do to help you?"

"I'm afraid to go home. I'm sure someone's waiting for me there. I don't know where to go. I just came from visiting some friends and I could have asked them to let me sleep there, but I think the police, or whoever else is after me, may know their address."

"Do you want to sleep here?"

"I didn't have the nerve to ask . . ."

"It's no problem. There's plenty of room."

"I don't know how to thank you."

"Jules, I'm always surrounded by people who are the same in all countries. They're very rich, they sometimes love music a little, but mainly they love success. Those people would never do anything for a young artist. They wait till you've become a star. They want you to be capricious, temperamental, even cruel, because it amuses them. Not one of them is interested in what I really am, not one of them loves music passionately. I know there are people who really care about me, but either I never meet them at all, or else I see them just long enough to autograph a program."

Jules looked at Cynthia, thinking only of her, forgetting the carpets, the mirrors, the paintings, that whole world of luxury which had overawed him at first.

"I understand," he said.

"That's why I like you to be here. That's why you can stay. I recognize real people right away."

They talked far into the night. When they became tired, she gave him a pillow and some blankets. He lay down on one of the sofas and quickly feel asleep. Cynthia stood looking at him for a moment, then she kissed him on the forehead and went to bed.

Gorodish had just found Simon Weinstadt's phone number. It was a little early to call him, but it would be better to get him when he was just out of bed. The phone rang a long time. Finally someone picked up.

"Hello."

"Mr. Weinstadt?"

"No. I can't disturb Mr. Weinstadt at this hour," replied the angelic voice of a young man. "Can you call back at ten o'clock?"

"It's very important."

"I'm his private secretary. Maybe you can tell me what it's about."

"It's about an excellent tape of Cynthia Hawkins' last concert that's in my possession."

"Hold on, please."

A minute later, Gorodish heard the voice of a man who had just waked up and was trying to give the impression that he had been working for at least two hours.

"My secretary tells me you have a tape of Miss Hawkins' last concert."

"That's right."

"A good tape would interest me but I don't think

yours is worth anything, except as a souvenir, since I didn't see any microphones on the stage. Furthermore it's illegal. It's a cassette, I suppose?"

"If you want technical details, I can tell you that the tape was made with a Nagra. The microphone was quite close to Miss Hawkins."

"Really? In that case..."

"I suggest that we listen to it together."

"I'm willing. Can you meet me in a private recording studio at Sixty-eight Rue de Seine, in the basement?"

"I'll be glad to. I live near there. Shall we say in half an hour?"

"Yes. Half an hour."

Gorodish was on his guard. He had the feeling that Weinstadt could be a formidable opponent. He walked to the studio. This time he didn't look like someone out for a stroll.

When he saw Weinstadt, his impression was confirmed. Gorodish would have to play his cards close to the vest.

They went into a room together to listen to the tape. Gorodish gave it to a technician after making sure that no copy of it would be made. Weinstadt was cold but polite. Silence.

When the first Schubert lied began, Weinstadt turned pale. This wasn't a tape made by a bungling amateur, as he had feared. He said nothing, pretended to be straining his ears and grimaced slightly at the sound of a barely audible cough. His heartbeat was quickening. He had realized that this would make one of the records of the century. He had to take a tough approach from the start.

He was silent till the tape ended, then he turned to Gorodish and said, "The recording isn't perfect, but it's acceptable. It's a long way from what could have been done in a studio."

"Maybe so, but it's the only one on the market."

"You want to sell it?"

"Yes. That's the purpose of our meeting."

"You realize, of course, that the tape won't have any real value unless Miss Hawkins authorizes its commercial use. Otherwise it's only a collector's item. I'm willing to make you a reasonable offer for it, even though it's highly unlikely that Miss Hawkins will allow it to be made public. I've known her for several years, I'm her exclusive agent for Europe, and I've often had occasion to offer her recording contracts. She's rejected them all. She mistrusts recordings, to put it mildly. I think she'll refuse this time too. But, as I said, I'm willing to take the risk of buying the tape from you."

"How much will you offer me?"

Weinstadt was thoughtful for a moment. He was beginning to think Gorodish must be greedy.

"Let's say twenty thousand francs."

"I don't think we understand each other very well. Let me tell you clearly how I see this operation. Now that you've heard the tape, I'd like you to get in touch with the record companies, just to let them know it's for sale. They'll make offers for it, we can count on that. You'll act as the go-between—that's your job, I believe—and you'll be paid your usual percentage."

"You're forgetting that without me it's impossible to get Miss Hawkins' consent, and that without her consent the record companies won't make any offers. You can always go to a pirate company, of course, but they're not easy to find and their funds are limited. Considering the circumstances, it seems to me that it would be fairer for us to divide the money between us. Neither of us can do anything without the other; together, we can do everything. That's the basis of a good partnership, don't you agree?"

Gorodish smiled amiably and was silent a long time, which seemed to disconcert Weinstadt.

"What makes you think I can't persuade Cynthia Hawkins to sign a contract?" Gorodish finally asked.

"I know her."

"Give me time to try. If I fail, I'll consider your proposition. But I have an important advantage that you don't know about. I'll succeed."

"I'm her adviser and she gives great weight to my opinion. She trusts me."

"I'm glad to hear it. Let's meet again in a few days. Meanwhile, I'll start the bids going on my own. You'll be surprised."

"I don't think you can succeed. Like all closed worlds, the music business has its own customs and conventions, and you don't know its accepted financial practices. You're an outsider. If I say the tape is good, the record companies will take my word for it. You'll have to prove it because they don't know you. And, as I said, the tape has imperfections. If I'm involved in the operation, no one will have any misgivings and the bids will be higher from the start."

Still smiling, Gorodish went to the technician's booth, took the tape, and carefully put it back in its box. He knew Weinstadt was watching him and beginning to lose a little of his self-assurance. This was no time to let down his guard. He went back to the impresario and said in a neutral tone, "I'm sorry my offer doesn't interest you now, but I think you'll want to discuss it again later."

Weinstadt was distressed at the idea that the tape might reach the market without having gone by way of him. He didn't think Gorodish would succeed, but he couldn't be sure.

"Let's try to come to an agreement," he said, looking unhappy. "It's important to act quickly in this kind of transaction. Give me a reasonable percentage and I don't think you'll regret it."

"Your usual commission is ten percent, isn't it?"

"Yes."

"I'll give you fifteen. That's my last offer."

"I'll take it, for the sake of music."

"It seems we both love music."

"A voice like Cynthia's is unique."

"I'll call you tonight and we'll see how things have developed by then. Can you have a contract drawn up?"

"Yes, of course."

They left the recording studio and went their separate ways.

It was hard for Weinstadt to keep his feelings under control. He was excited by the discovery that there was an excellent tape of Cynthia's best concert, and elated at the prospect of making a tidy sum for himself and increasing his prestige.

By the time he had walked home, his plan was ready. He picked up the phone. It didn't matter what order he made his calls in.

Fifteen minutes later, representatives of DGG, Philips, Decca, RCA, EMI, and Nippon Columbia knew about the tape. None of them had asked to hear it. Weinstadt had said it was exceptionally good.

Panic spread among the representatives. Telexes were sent to Hamburg, Amsterdam, London, New

York, and Tokyo to ask how much could be bid.

An hour later, the DGG representative received a telex in answer to his: NO LIMIT. WE WANT AN EXCLUSIVE CONTRACT WITH THAT ARTIST.

Meanwhile Jules was having an English-style breakfast with his Diva. He had forgotten his danger and the police. They talked about opera and Cynthia was amazed at the extent of his knowledge.

When they had finished the eggs, toast, and jam, she ordered more tea.

"What are you doing today?" asked Jules.

"I'm going to practice a little, as I do every morning. Then I'm having lunch with the director of the Paris Opéra to discuss plans. This afternoon I'll go to a couturier to have one or two dresses made; I've seen some very beautiful ones that I want. I expect to be back by the end of the afternoon."

"I'm afraid to go out during the day. Can I stay here till night? I'll leave by the back door."

"Do as you please. As far as I'm concerned, there's no problem. I only wish I didn't have all those appointments."

"I'll wait for you."

"Come, I'll run a bubble bath for you, and I'll practice while you're taking it."

"Can I leave the door open?"

"If you like. I always practice alone, you know, in my negligee. I've never let anyone hear me before."

Jules got into the bathtub, leaned back, and stretched out his legs. The sound of his Diva's voice made him tremble with happiness.

Saporta had become incapable of clipping off the ends of his Havana cigars with his teeth, as he usually did. He was so nervous that he ruined a cigar each time he tried it.

Not only was he getting nowhere at all, but even the cops, who were his allies in this situation, had failed to get their hands on that damned RCA messenger. Saporta still had a faint hope that the messenger would pay a visit to one of the whores on the Avenue Foch. Their pimps had ordered them to be on the lookout for him; there was a lot of money to be made by catching him.

The Hôtel George-V had become a communications center where Saporta was kept posted from hour to hour. What infuriated him was that nothing seemed to be happening even though he had men everywhere. Their orders were simple: get the cassette, by any means necessary. Saporta didn't care who had to be killed to do it.

He took all his meals at the hotel, in the company of his favorite killers. Ever since finding out about the cassette, he hadn't even felt like laying any of the enticing women who were at his disposal night and day. His anxiety was becoming unbearable. At night he dreamed of spiders and horrible insects crawling all over him, while sickening liquids oozed from green blisters that covered his whole body.

Between phone calls, the room was silent. Paulo and Louis cleaned and oiled their artillery as quietly as if they were in a funeral parlor.

Since the Japanese were prepared to pay out mountains of yen to get the tape of Cynthia Hawkins concert, they weren't too worried. Yet Tsukahara wanted to continue his amateur detective work. It would be safer that way. His competitors also had money, and in this kind of duel you could never be sure who was going to come out on top.

After he and his colleague had received their telex from Tokyo and called Weinstadt to say they were willing to pay a large price, without specifying the exact amount, they went to have lunch at the Osaka Restaurant. Then, at three o'clock, they began lurking outside the Ritz, hoping to make direct contact with the man who had recorded the tape.

They hadn't noticed that a car had been discreetly following them ever since they left their hotel. In that car sat Paula, who was acting on intuition, with three police inspectors to keep her company.

Jules had dinner with his Diva that evening. They stayed in her suite and ate one of the chef's specialties, foie gras with port wine, followed by a delicious rib of beef. They talked awhile after the meal, then Jules decided it was time for him to try to slip out of the Ritz unseen. Cynthia made him promise to come back if he had any problems, and kissed him on the forehead when he left. A little later, she was surprised to find herself thinking about him with anxiety.

Jules had called for a taxi. It was waiting for him when he came out of the Ritz. He got into it and gave the driver an address near the place where he had left his motorbike. The Japanese started off behind him. They had been waiting eight hours. The cops' Peugeot brought up the rear. The little procession passed the Place de la Concorde and headed for the Boulevard Saint-Germain.

Jules, who had seen detective movies, knew you were supposed to keep checking to see if you were being followed. He did it, at first only as a kind of game, but then he realized he had been seeing the same blue Toyota for several minutes. His fear came rushing back to him. He would have to make a fast getaway when the taxi stopped. He took out the key to the padlock on his motorbike, to have it ready, then he paid the driver in advance with a generous tip, and told him to speed up and pass as many other cars as he could.

The Japanese saw the taxi suddenly pull away from them. Since they knew more about music than driving, they had a hard time following it. Soon there were several cars between them and Jules.

The cops realized they would have to pass the Japanese to keep from losing the messenger. While the Toyota resounded with Oriental curses, the Peugeot pulled alongside it and quickly left it in the dust.

Jules jumped out of the taxi like a kangaroo. After the three agonizing seconds it took him to open the padlock, he pushed his motorbike as fast as he could, to get it started. The motor was beginning to cough when the cops turned on their siren and he saw a black car bearing down on him.

It came to a sudden stop. A scene from *2001* flashed into his mind when he saw the doors fly open and cops come tumbling out. They ran toward him, dashing through the traffic as if they were bent on suicide. There were sounds of brakes screeching and cars being rammed from the rear. Just then the motor of Jules' bike came to life. He leaped onto the seat and took off down the street. The cops hurried back to their car and drove after him.

He saw the window of Le Drugstore and people standing inside. They seemed to be staring at him.

On the Rue de Rennes he looked back and saw the police car close behind him. At the rate it was going, it would catch him in a few seconds. He had to do something. He turned right, into the Rue Bernard-Palissy, a narrow little street that wouldn't have been out of place in the Middle Ages. The cops came after him, sideswiping a parked car that stuck out a little too far into the street. Jules felt as if the Peugeot were breathing down his neck. It was time to get off this street.

He turned into another one, whose name he didn't know. The cops passed a slow-moving car and picked up speed. They were determined to get that little bastard.

Jules headed for Montparnasse. He rode along a one-way street in the wrong direction and begged his guardian angels to send a big truck down the middle of it, but they ignored him. Then he turned toward the Tour Montparnasse skyscraper, which was almost as high as it was ugly. Since there was some fairly heavy traffic, he pulled fifty yards farther ahead of the Peugeot. He had just run a red light and was wondering where to go next when his sluggish angels finally shook off their apathy and whispered into his ear that he should shift course in the direction of Maître Kanter's restaurant. He let himself be guided by the divine voices.

The cops had picked up a few more dents in their car but they couldn't have cared less about that. They bulled their way through the traffic and gained a little ground. They thought Jules was going to take the Rue d'Odessa, but they got the surprise of their lives.

Again it was the angels who told Jules where to go, and he obeyed them. He heard, "Ride down the stairs of the subway station."

He rode down them. He hadn't been shaken like

that since his father caught him stealing the grocery money when he was fifteen.

The cops stopped their car, left it where it was, and ran down the stairs. One of them sprained his ankle just as Jules pushed open a door with the front wheel of his motorbike.

He rode down another flight of stairs and sped along a corridor with people coming toward him from the opposite direction while the cops ran after him for all they were worth. He saw people flattening themselves against the white walls. He felt as if he were in a big bathroom.

He came to the conveyor belt that led to the railroad station. He took the passageway beside it, glanced over his shoulder, and saw one of the police inspectors behind him. He didn't think the cop could keep up that pace to the end of the passageway, and he couldn't catch him even if he did, because his motorbike was gathering speed now. He was probably doing at least thirty miles an hour. He heard shouts and saw people get down on the floor. Shit! Were the cops going to start shooting?

He reached the foot of the stairs leading back up to the street. Impossible to ride his motorbike up them. As he was about to abandon his faithful companion, he remembered that the gloves Alba had given him were in the saddlebag. He looked back. The cop was still far away. Jules reached into the saddlebag and took out, besides his gloves, a Memorex cassette. He put it in his jacket pocket.

Now that he was off his motorbike, he was in the same situation as the cop, except that he wasn't out of breath. He climbed the stairs in a few big leaps. Instead of going out onto the esplanade, where he was afraid he might get an unpleasant surprise, he ran to the taxi stand. Only one cab was waiting there. He got into it.

"Hurry! My girlfriend's husband is after me! He wants to kill me!"

The amused driver took off at full speed. Jules turned around and saw the police inspector come charging into the middle of the street.

"Don't worry," said the driver, who had looked in the rearview mirror, "there's no other cab back there. He's stranded."

CHAPTER SEVEN

JULES SUDDENLY REALIZED THAT HE DIDN'T know where to go. No place was safe for him now. His address was known, he had been followed when he left the Ritz, Alba and Gorodish were probably being watched, he couldn't go to any hotel, and he had lost his motorbike.

He had the horrible feeling of being crushed in a vise. And he still couldn't understand why all this was happening to him.

"Where shall I take you?" asked the driver.

Jules vainly tried to think of a possible refuge. Nothing seemed safe to him. He was a prisoner in that taxi. If it hadn't been for his motorbike, the cops would already have arrested him. He knew Paris like the palm of his hand, and that motorbike had been almost a part of him. He would have to find another one. For a moment he considered stealing one, but that would be a useless risk. He began thinking over the other messengers he knew. He was on good terms with some of them. The taxi was approaching the Porte d'Orléans which marked the boundary between the city and suburbs. He saw a phone booth.

"Let me off here," he told the driver.

As soon as he got out of the taxi he felt that he was no longer safe. His anxiety flared up whenever anyone looked at him. He kept watching all around him, ready to run away at the slightest sign of anything suspicious.

He was so jittery that when he opened the phone book he seemed to have forgotten the letters of the alphabet. Finally he found a friend's name and dialed the number.

"Hello, this is Jules."

"You just woke me up from a terrific dream."

"Can you do me a favor? I'm in big trouble."

"What's wrong?"

"I can't explain now, but I need a motorbike right away."

"For how long?"

"A day, maybe two, no more."

"Then I can't let you have mine because I'm working tomorrow. But I can lend you my motor-cycle."

"Is it a big one?"

"It's a Yamaha Trial 125."

Jules was beginning to breathe more easily.

"Look, I really appreciate this," he said. "If there's ever anything I can do for you . . . I have to ask you one more favor; can you bring it to me at the Porte d'Orléans? I'm afraid to come to your place."

"How will I get back home?"

"I'll give you money for a taxi."

"Okay. Where shall I meet you?"

"Just come to the Porte d'Orléans and I'll see you."

"I'll be right there."

Jules stayed in the phone booth a long time before daring to venture outside. He was afraid to go into a café or walk along the street because he might be spotted by cops. He went into the courtyard of a building and waited.

All the police cars in Paris had been given Jules' description and were cruising all over the city, looking for him. Everyone wearing jeans and a leather jacket was stopped. Boulanger, Paula, and the whole Vice Squad were up in arms.

Jules came out of the courtyard. A few minutes later his friend arrived and turned the motorcycle over to him. Jules quickly gave him money for a taxi and rode off toward the *périphérique*, the highway that circled Paris. The cops weren't likely to be looking for him there. It was a little cold. He put on his gloves. It occurred to him that he could leave Paris and hide out somewhere in the country. But where? He didn't know anyone he trusted who lived in the country. He decided to ride on the *périphérique* till he got an idea.

When he saw the sign announcing the Porte Dauphine, he got his idea: Karina. If she would let him spend the night with her, he was saved. He left the *périphérique* and started along the Avenue Foch. Suddenly a black wall appeared in his mind. He had only a hundred francs on him. He was sure Karina wouldn't give him a whole night for that. But since he couldn't think of any other way to solve his problem, he decided to try his luck with her.

He slowed down when he came to her part of the street, trembling at the thought that she might have gone off with a customer.

When he had passed five or six other women, he

saw Karina waving to him. She was wearing tiny leather shorts and high black boots.

"I'm glad you came back," she said. "I've thought about you often."

"Me too. I've come to see if you'd do me a favor. I hate to ask it of you, but I have no choice. The cops are looking for me, I have nowhere to go, and I've only got a hundred francs. I thought maybe I could spend the night with you. I'll give you the rest of the money next time, if it's all right with you."

"Don't be so upset. I don't mind waiting for the money. The only problem is my man. If I don't give him enough money tomorrow, he'll beat me to a pulp. So here's what we'll do: I'll go on working till three in the morning and you'll wait for me in my apartment. I'll give you the keys. I can take my customers to a hotel. Do you remember where I live?"

"I remember the building, but not which floor you're on."

"Fourth floor, the door on the right. Here are the keys."

Jules kissed Karina.

"Please come as soon as you can," he said. "Being alone is going to make me nervous."

"You'll only have to wait a couple of hours."

He rode along the silent, deserted little streets, parked his motorcycle on the sidewalk, and went into Karina's building.

Karina walked to the nearest café, feeling as if she were about to vomit. For a moment she had an impulse to run back and warn Jules, but she regretfully decided against it when she remembered what Saporta had done to some women she knew who hadn't followed his orders.

She bought a phone token from the cashier in the café and went down to the basement. Never in her life had she felt such disgust for herself. She reached into her purse for the number she had been given and took a deep breath before dialing it.

"Hôtel George-V."

"Room 103, please."

"Saporta here."

"This is Karina. He's in my apartment."

"Good. Go back to work. We'll get in touch with you tomorrow."

Saporta hung up.

When he took off his jacket, Jules remembered the cassette he had put in his pocket. He looked at it, thinking it was one of his own recordings. Since he had to kill time while he waited for Karina, he put the cassette on her player, turned it on and sat down to listen.

As soon as he heard the first few words, he was chilled by the sound of Nadia's voice. After identifying herself, she briefly described her life and told how she had met Saporta, then she predicted that her disappearance or death would be discovered before long, and accused Saporta of it in advance.

Next, in a neutral tone, like someone dictating a letter, she began giving the names of people who worked for Saporta in his prostitution network. She specified each one's job and the sector he was responsible for. After a detailed description of the call-girl operation and the houses specializing in juvenile prostitutes, she listed the public places of prostitution that were under Saporta's control.

Jules suddenly felt as if his heart were about to explode. The voice on the cassette had said, "All the black prostitutes who work on the Avenue Victor-Hugo, the Rue de Presbourg, and the Avenue Foch are under Saporta's direct control."

Jules leaped to his feet, took the cassette, put on his jacket, and ran down the stairs. He had just understood why he was being hunted. He didn't know how that cassette had gotten into his saddlebag, but everything else was clear.

As he was about to leave the building, he heard a car stop in front of it. He hesitated a second and saw a door that looked as if it might lead into a storeroom or a cellar. He opened it, stepped inside, and pulled it shut behind him, after catching a glimpse of two men coming into the entrance hall. He heard them hurry up the stairs. He waited a few moments while he caught his breath, then he silently came out and went down the front steps.

Saporta and Paulo had gone upstairs, carrying .38 pistols with silencers. Louis stayed at the wheel of the Mercedes. He had just parked between two other cars when he saw Jules leave the building and get on a motorcycle.

Louis quickly took his gun from the glove compartment. As soon as he had finished screwing on the silencer, he heard the motorcycle roar. He jumped out of the Mercedes. Jules was already off to a fast start. He was hundred feet away when the first shot made the dull sound of a soccer ball dropped on the ground. Louis emptied his pistol.

Saporta and Paulo came bursting out of the building and plunged into the Mercedes while Louis was firing his last shot. Paulo took the wheel. He backed up, crashing into the Volkswagen behind him, shifted, and took off.

Jules felt a sharp pain in his leg. The shock staggered him for a moment. He swerved, grazed a truck with his shoulder, then managed to straighten out the motorcycle. He heard the crunch of the mangled Volkswagen, followed by the shriek of tires protesting against the violent acceleration of the Mercedes.

He raced toward the Avenue Foch, while Saporta, leaning out the window of the Mercedes, fired his pistol into the night.

Jules crossed the little park beside the Avenue Foch, weaving to avoid the benches and trees. When he flew off the sidewalk and into the street, he barely missed the tide of oncoming cars that had just been freed by a green light. He lifted his front wheel to go up onto the other sidewalk and soon vanished into the darkness of the little side streets while Saporta's Mercedes stopped in front of a stubborn tree that wouldn't let it pass.

This was the first time Paulo had ever seen his boss lose his self-control. It would have taken a whole handful of tranquilizers to calm him.

Saporta picked up the phone in his car and gave orders for all his men to go into action. Within half an hour, the city was being crisscrossed by gangsters who had been told to shoot Jules on sight.

When Jules was sure he had thrown the Mercedes off his trail, he stopped on a quiet street to examine his wound. The bullet had gone through his calf, making an ugly, bloody hole. He made a tourniquet with his handkerchief, then tried to think.

He was sure of one thing: the cops wanted to

arrest him and the gangsters wanted to kill him. Trembling all over, barely able to stand, he mentally wrestled with the problem of where he could go to be safe. He had decided to leave the motorcycle somewhere but he had to find a taxi.

He slowly rode to the Place du Trocadéro. He felt his nerves and muscles abandoning him, and his body seemed to be liquefying.

He had to call Gorodish. He was the only one who could save him. Jules went into a phone booth and dialed the number. Alba answered.

"This is Jules. I . . ." His voice failed him.

"What's the matter? Are you tired from spending too much time with your singer?"

"Alba, they tried to kill me! I'm wounded! I understand everything now. Serge has to help me, or they'll get me for sure."

"Are you talking about the cops?"

"No, gangsters."

"Is your wound serious? Where is it?"

"In my leg. I think I'll be all right."

Gorodish, who had been listening to Alba's end of the conversation, stood up from the sofa and took the receiver from her hand.

"Are you bleeding very much?"

"I slowed it down by tying a handkerchief around my leg."

"Can you take a taxi?"

"Yes."

"Then listen to me carefully. Have the driver let you off at the back door of Le Drugstore de l'Etoile. Go to the pharmacy section and buy some cotton, some alcohol, and a bandage. Go upstairs to the bathroom, disinfect your wound, bandage it tightly, and stay put till I get there. There's a bullet hole in your pants leg, right?"

"Yes, and there's blood on it too."

"It won't be easy not to attract attention, but do your best. Try to walk without limping. If the pharmacy section is too crowded, go straight up to the bathroom and I'll bring you what you need. Keep your chin up. I'll get there as fast as I can."

Jules got into a taxi and gave the address of Le Drugstore de l'Etoile. They passed a slow-moving police car. He was afraid he wouldn't be able to get out of the taxi.

Mohammed was asleep when Gorodish called. Gorodish told him to come immediately and have his taxi's gas tank filled on the way. Meanwhile Alba was getting dressed. She nearly put her jeans on backward.

Gorodish took a pair of pants, a sweater, and a tweed jacket for Jules. He had to change his appearance.

Alba's throat was so tight she couldn't say a word. Serge put his arm around her in the elevator.

"Don't worry, we'll take care of him."

They waited in front of the building. Since Mohammed lived in the Bastille quarter, it would take him awhile to get there.

Gorodish realized he had forgotten something. He went back up to the apartment, put his old American .45 automatic in his coat pocket and rejoined Alba.

Each time Jules took a step with his left foot, pain jolted his leg. He went into the pharmacy section of Le Drugstore de l'Etoile, made an effort to smile, and asked for what he needed. A young woman served him with indifference.

He went up to the bathroom. His forehead was

covered with cold sweat. He was afraid someone had noticed his wounded leg. As soon as he had closed the bathroom door behind him, his nervous tension made him burst out sobbing. It was a good five minutes before he was able to roll up his pants leg, disinfect his wound, wipe off the blood, and put on a bandage. Then he waited, terrified each time he heard the slightest sound. He kept repeating to himself, "Serge is coming, Serge is coming."

Everything was confused in his mind. How had that cassette gotten into the saddlebag of his motorbike? How did the police and the gangsters know he had it? Why weren't the police protecting him? These unanswered questions seemed to plunge him into a world of total absurdity.

It had been easy for Kazuhichi Tsukahara and his colleague from Nippon Columbia to make a connection between Jules, Alba, and Gorodish. They were convinced that the man they had seen in the street, with Alba or alone, was responsible for Weinstadt's putting the Cynthia Hawkins tape up for sale. What they didn't understand was why the police were so interested in Jules. They thought he must be mixed up in something outside the music business but they didn't know what it might be.

The head of the Japanese firm still hoped to have an advantage over his competitors. To give himself time to finish his investigation, he had made a substantial offer and told Weinstadt he was prepared to discuss raising it if higher offers were received.

Tsukahara had soon realized that he was much better at supervising recordings than doing detective work, so he had called Tokyo and asked them to recommend a specialist.

The man recommended to him was a Japanese

living in France. Tsukahara wasn't told anything very specific about him only that he was qualified to carry out a delicate investigation.

Tsukahara had given him Alba and Gorodish's address. He knew Alba was a minor and he suspected Gorodish of having illicit relations with her. The agent was to find out for sure. If Tsukahara was right, he would have a means of putting pressure on Gorodish. He had also told the agent to look carefully into Gorodish's whole past.

Though it was late at night, Tsukahara couldn't sleep. As he conscientiously got himself drunk on sake, he thought of the record jacket that would have three names on it: Cynthia Hawkins, Kazuhichi Tsukahara, and Nippon Columbia.

Jules' heart jumped into his throat when he heard a knock on the door. Serge's voice immediately reassured him. He opened the door. Serge handed him the clothes he had brought.

Jules changed into them. He was beginning to hope, but they still had to get out of Paris.

He looked at himself in a mirror, rinsed his face with warm water, and put his jeans and leather jacket into the bag that Serge gave him. They went downstairs and left by the back door.

When Jules sat down in the taxi between Serge and Alba, he felt great relief. Gorodish had asked him not to talk in front of Mohammed, so they rode in silence. Mohammed drove out of the city and took a highway going south.

Alba held Jules' hand and he rested his head on her shoulder. Gorodish kept his eyes open. He looked back several times to make sure they weren't being followed.

Two hours later, he got out to open a gate and

the taxi then rolled along an unpaved driveway through spacious grounds. Alba recognized the high grass, the big tree, and the silhouette of Serge's house in the darkness. That house was his refuge, the place where he had taken her after throwing her hometown into turmoil.

They went inside. While Alba made hot bouillon, Gorodish lit a big fire in the living-room fireplace. Then they moved a battered old sofa close to the fire, and there, wrapped in blankets, Jules gave them a detailed account of everything that had happened to him since he left them the night before.

Alba went up to Serge's room and brought down a cassette player. They listened to the cassette all the way through. Gorodish was dumbfounded. They were sitting on a keg of gunpowder. The only positive point was that Gorodish knew Saporta. He had been his chauffeur during the period of his youth when he was more or less involved in the underworld. In those days, Saporta had been only at the beginning of his career, but Gorodish had never doubted that he would go far.

He said nothing about all this to Jules and Alba.

"They won't give up till they find us," said Jules.

"Don't worry. I'll work something out."

Alba had imagined having exciting adventures with Serge, but till now the possibility of risking her life had never been real to her. Jules had nearly been killed. He had escaped only by a miracle.

Gorodish examined Jules' wound and rebandaged it. The bullet had gone through his calf without striking bone. It was painful, but not dangerous.

Gorodish gave him an antibiotic and a sedative. Alba put Jules to bed and got into her own bed soon after.

GORODISH SAT BY THE FIRE WITH HIS .45 AUTO-matic beside him on the sofa. Anything could happen. He had to be ready

The first glow of dawn began lighting the living room. A rooster crowed. The sound made Gorodish feel better.

A little before eight o'clock he made himself a cup of black coffee and decided to go back to Paris with the cassette. He had to act quickly. Keeping that cassette very long would mean certain death. He had decided to contact Saporta.

He went up to Alba's room. She was still sound asleep. He sat down on the big bed and gently stroked her forehead till she woke up.

"I'm going to Paris and taking the cassette with me. We have to get rid of it. Take care of Jules. I'll call you. I hope I can come back and take you away from here tomorrow."

Alba nodded and went back to sleep.

Gorodish took out the keys and registration papers of his Peugeot station wagon and got into it, with his .45 and the cassette. After some trouble getting the engine started, he drove off toward Paris.

When he reached the Rue de l'Université, everything seemed calm. He parked and went up to the apartment. He turned on the coffee maker, put in enough water and ground coffee for ten cups, and settled into his reclining chair. He knew the slightest mistake could be fatal.

He was sipping a cup of delicious pure Colombian coffee when the phone rang.

"Is this Serge Gorodish?"

"Yes. Who are you?"

"I'm Alba's father."

Gorodish had completely forgotten that Alba had a father. At the same time, he remembered that he hadn't sent him his monthly check.

"How are you?" he asked.

"I'm fine, thanks. Are you satisfied with the way Alba has been studying?"

"I'm amazed at her progress. She's learning even faster than I expected. I'm sure she'll go far. Incidentally, I just realized I haven't sent you this month's check yet. I'll do it today."

"There's no rush, Mr. Gorodish. That's not why I called you. I want to tell you about a strange visit I had. A Japanese gentleman came to give me a free calculator. He said his company was giving them away as part of an advertising campaign. I was glad to have it. We started talking and I told him about my children. I said Alba was very gifted, and was studying in Paris. He said he'd like to give her a present too, since Paris was part of his territory. He asked me how old she was and if she was in a boarding school. I told him she lived with her guardian. It wasn't till after he'd left that I started thinking there was something funny about the way he pumped me for information. So I decided to call you. You never know . . ."

Gorodish realized that things were becoming more complicated. He thanked Alba's father, promised to visit him soon, and said he was sorry Alba wasn't there to talk to him because she had gone to her class in Indian dancing.

That story about the Japanese reminded him that he had to call Weinstadt. He dialed his number.

"How's the bidding going, Mr. Weinstadt?"

"Nothing's settled yet, but I've already had some good offers: three hundred thousand francs from Philips, four hundred thousand from Nippon Columbia. From a financial, promotional, and artistic viewpoint, though, I think DGG's offer is the most interesting. They haven't named a price but they say they're determined to outbid everyone else, provided Miss Hawkins agrees to an exclusive contract and a recording program spread over five years. I think we have to wait awhile. The contracts are ready. With luck, we can close the deal in a few days."

"Has Miss Hawkins agreed to it in principle?"

"I haven't talked to her about it yet. I'm waiting for DGG's definitive offer."

"All right, I'll call you later."

Gorodish went back to his reclining chair and continued examining the situation. If the Japanese were delving into his present life, they were probably also delving into his past. They wanted the tape and they were looking for a way to blackmail him. He had two tapes that were worth a fortune. All he had to do was stay alive to spend it. The whole thing would have to be settled within two days. The problem was how. Circuits began clicking in his brain.

Again the phone rang, and again it was Alba's father.

"He came back. This time I acted stupid. I didn't tell him anything he wanted to know and I found out something about him. He's staying at the Hôtel de la Grande Chasse here, and he's going back to Paris this evening. I don't trust him. If he comes to you and tries to sell you something, don't buy it. I read an article that said you should always be on your guard when a salesman gives you something for free, so be careful with that Japanese. Whatever he's selling may be expensive junk."

"I'll take your advice. If he comes here, I won't let him in the door. By the way, what did you talk about with him?"

"Like I said, I didn't tell him anything he wanted to know. I just told him about the things that happened in our town not long ago: the murders, the Vampire gang, the bank robbery, all that. They're still the favorite subjects here, you know. People always come back to them when they don't have anything else to talk about."

"Thanks for calling. We'll come to see you soon."

Gorodish hung up. Things were becoming even more complicated than he'd thought. That Japanese was starting to get on his nerves.

Half an hour later, the phone rang once again.

"Mr. Gorodish?"

"Yes."

"I don't have the honor of knowing you but I'd like to meet you soon because Nippon Columbia has asked me to negotiate a contract with you for the sale of a certain tape."

"I'm not handling that matter directly. I've turned it over to Miss Hawkins' agent, whom I'm sure you know. You can discuss it with him."

"We've been in touch with Mr. Weinstadt, but I have a proposition for you that I think you'll find more interesting than anything the other record companies have to offer."

"As I've already told you, only Simon Weinstadt is in a position to give you an answer to your proposition," Gorodish said coldly, still pretending to be dense.

"I don't think you understand the nature of my proposition, Mr. Gorodish. It concerns you personally because I've learned certain things which I believe are important enough to stop the rapid rise in the price of your tape. We're willing to pay a reasonable sum, of course, but no more. I want to meet you as soon as possible to settle the terms of our agreement."

"I have a full day ahead of me. I can see you either in an hour or late this evening."

"I prefer this evening."

"Let's say eleven o'clock, then, at my apartment."

"Very well, Mr. Gorodish."

The blackmailer's choice of a later meeting confirmed what Alba's father had reported: he wasn't leaving the small town till evening. There was probably something else he still wanted to discover, to increase the pressure he could put on Serge.

Gorodish poured himself a seventh cup of coffee, turned on his stereo and began listening to Alfred Brendel's rendition of Beethoven's Sonata opus 10 no. 1. At difficult times, he needed to be completely calm.

* * *

Alba woke up and stretched like a cat. She wondered what time it was. Late, probably. The house
was silent. She lay looking up at the ceiling, reliving
the wonderful moments she had spent in that house.
Then, wanting to see the big cedar tree, she got up
and opened the shutters. That was when she remembered Serge's departure. Since she was naked,
she wrapped herself in the bedspread before going
to see Jules, who had slept in Serge's room.

He was still asleep. Alba opened the shutters and
looked at him. He was evidently dreaming, because
his mouth and eyelids were quivering.

She lifted the covers and lay down beside him in
the big bed, without taking off her bedspread. She
let him go on sleeping. With her head on the fragrant pillow, she thought of everything that had
happened since the day when they met each other
in Lido-Musique: the evening they had spent together, the music, his kisses... Then she thought
of Serge, of his apparent coldness and the rare moments when he let himself go. She wondered if he
loved her as she loved him. And she wondered why
he didn't really treat her as a woman, why he didn't
take her in his arms more often, and kiss her the
way she wanted him to. He didn't seem to notice
all her signals, all her carefully planned efforts to
entice him. None of them worked. She thought he
might love another woman. But she was a woman
too, and wanted to prove it. She turned these things
over in her mind a long time without finding any
answers that satisfied her. Maybe Serge felt she was
too young. She touched her little breasts and made
them stick out farther by squeezing her shoulders
toward each other. They would get bigger, she was

sure of that, but she wondered how long she would have to wait. Then she remembered the African creams and lotions she had seen advertised in magazines.

She got up, went down to the living room, took a pile of magazines, and began looking for the ad she had seen so often. When she found it, she tore off the address at the bottom of the page, opened the dusty writing desk, and took out an envelope, a sheet of paper, and a ball-point pen. In her best handwriting, she ordered five jars of the African cream that produced amazing results, according to the ad. She hoped that with its help she would finally get Serge to see her as a real woman and act accordingly.

She put her letter in the envelope, addressed it, and slipped it into a pocket of the jacket she had tossed onto a chair. She went upstairs and got back in bed beside Jules. He had finished his dream.

She wanted him to kiss her as he had done in his apartment. She loved that kind of kiss. It left her body hot and trembling, as if she had a fever. She heard a blackbird singing and it reminded her of Cynthia Hawkins. She knew Jules was in love with that woman. His dreams had probably been about her. This thought cooled Alba's body and mind. She got out of bed and went down to make breakfast with whatever she could find in the kitchen.

Luckily the cupboard wasn't bare. There was banana Nesquik, coffee, chocolate, English jam, crackers, and condensed milk. Since she thought Jules needed something strong to shake him loose from his dreams, she made coffee for him.

She put the breakfast on a tray, took it upstairs, set it down on the bed, and woke Jules in the most effective way she knew: by pinching his nostrils shut. After all, it wasn't her fault if he hadn't woken up at the right time.

He grunted unhappily at having been plunged directly into reality.

"It was mean of you to wake me up like that."

"I had to do it quickly, so your coffee wouldn't get cold."

Jules tried to sit up in bed. He had forgotten his wounded leg and the sudden movement made him cry out in pain.

"I'd forgotten about that. . . ."

"Did you sleep all right?"

"Yes, pretty well. Where's Serge?"

"In Paris. He left very early and took the cassette. He wants to get the whole thing settled."

"I hope there won't be any trouble. . . ."

"You don't know Serge," Alba said calmly, sipping her Nesquik.

"When's he coming back?" Jules asked with anxiety in his voice.

"Tomorrow, maybe. He said he'd call us."

"I can't help thinking about how those bastards nearly killed me. It gives you a funny feeling to have somebody shooting at you."

"It's not like being at a nice, safe concert, is it?"

Since Jules detected a certain acidity in this question, he didn't answer it. He began thinking of Cynthia. He imagined her in her suite at the Ritz and wondered if anyone had told her about the tape of her concert yet.

"What are you thinking about?" asked Alba.

"My motorbike. I had to leave it behind when the cops were chasing me. I hope I can get it back."

Alba finished off the jar of jam with her spoon. Men were such bad liars. . . .

"I have to change the cotton under your bandage," she said.

When she walked out of the room, the bedspread draped around her made her look like an actress in an ancient tragedy. She went downstairs and came back with a basin of hot water, a towel, cotton, and a bottle of alcohol.

Jules pulled the covers off his leg and lay back on the pillow. She put his heel on her thigh and unwrapped the bandage. The cotton was soaked with blood. When she saw his wound she felt sorry for poor Jules and decided she had treated him too harshly. He had always been very nice to her.

After washing and disinfecting his wound, she put the bandage back in place and helped him to slide his leg under the covers. She put the basin on the floor and got into the bed. Jules was sweating a little; the alcohol had burned terribly when she cleaned his wound with it, but he hadn't said anything. She wiped his forehead with the sheet. She took his hot cheeks between her cool hands and looked at him a long time, then she put her lips on his, opened her mouth and pressed up against him.

Gorodish had made at least a dozen calls to get Saporta's number. Finally, at the Hôtel George-V he was given the number of the phone in the Mercedes.

"Saporta here."

"I don't know if you remember me, but long ago I used to drive a light blue Chevrolet Impala for you."

"I remember you very well, Serge Gorodish."

"I have to talk to you as soon as possible."

"Can you wait a few days? I'm doing something that takes up all my time."

"That's exactly what I want to talk to you about."

"Where and when?"

"How about half an hour from now, on the third lower level of the parking garage across the street from the Brasserie Lipp?"

"Okay."

Gorodish took a shower to make himself more alert. He was beginning to feel the effects of his sleepless night.

He put on clean clothes and slipped his .45 into his belt, under his thick wool jacket. Before leaving the apartment, he hid the cassette in a record cabinet.

He had worked out his plan. Now he could only hope there wouldn't be any hitches.

CHAPTER NINE

GORODISH WALKED DOWN THE LITTLE STAIR-case leading to the lower levels of the parking garage. At the third level he opened the door and stepped into a long gray hall.

He looked to his left, saw a Mercedes with blinking headlights and went toward it. Its back door opened. A man got out and came forward to meet him. Gorodish didn't recognize him immediately. Saporta had changed a lot. Through the years, his face had taken on a look that was both more ferocious and more neutral. Nothing was the same except the smile that lifted only one corner of his lips.

They shook hands, each trying to gauge the other's strength, and looked at each other for long seconds.

"Let's get into the car," said Saporta. "We can talk better there."

They sat down in the back seat. Saporta ordered Louis to take a walk. He wanted to be alone with Gorodish.

"Serge, you're the only one who ever left me

without trying to go into competition with me afterward. I've always wondered if you really dropped out. I haven't heard anything about you since the night when we had our last dinner together."

"I dropped out, then came back in. Like a lot of people, I floundered awhile before I found my way. I wasn't like you: it didn't take you long to decide where you wanted to go."

"That's true. I was on the right track by the time I was fifteen. Who are you working for?"

"I work alone."

"How did you get the cassette?"

"By chance."

"That's strange," said Saporta, evidently not believing him.

"Yes, I think so too."

"Do you really have it?"

Gorodish didn't answer, but he raised his heavy eyelids and gave Saporta an icy look.

"All right, you have it," Saporta conceded, "and you want to sell it."

"I have a bank account in Switzerland and I haven't put anything into it for a long time. As you know, those banks make their foreign depositors pay negative interest."

Saporta took a Havana cigar from a leather case. He lit it self-consciously and looked at Gorodish with no expression in his eyes.

"How much do you want?"

"A million francs. Swiss francs, of course."

Saporta blew a long puff of fragrant smoke up to the ceiling of the car. He had been very nervous the last few days.

"Don't you think you're going a little too far?"

"You're free to refuse. And there's more. I also want you to have your men get rid of someone for me, a Japanese who's trying to pull something on me. He's in France. I don't think I'm asking too much for twenty years of freedom."

"I can offer you something better, in the long run. A partnership. Half and half."

"Look, you and I both have our habits. You've never had a partner and I'm used to working alone. Let's keep it that way."

"I'll need time to get the money together."

"That's only natural. I'll give you till midnight."

Saporta crushed his cigar in the ashtray. Not many people had ever talked to him like that, and those who had done it before were all dead.

"What if I can't pay you by then?"

"The cassette will be put in circulation."

"I can't stop you from doing that."

"You should know me better than to think I'd come to you like this without first making arrangements for the cassette to be delivered to the right people after a certain time. You can have me killed, but it wouldn't do you any good."

"Where is your Japanese?"

"In a little town not far away. He's supposed to come back to Paris this evening. Traffic is light on the road he'll take. I want it to look like an accident."

"So, besides wanting all that money, you're fussy about the way the job will be done...."

"You know you'll never hear from me again when this is over. You're lucky: you might have had to deal with someone less easygoing than I am."

"If the money is deposited to your account this afternoon and the Japanese is dead tonight, when will I get the cassette?"

"After the accident. We can meet on the same road, a little farther on."

"You're not afraid?"

"I don't have as many reasons to be afraid as you do. I've taken all kinds of precautions. If you want to know what I've been doing the last twenty years, I can tell you that I've specialized in my own line of work and mastered it almost completely. That's why you've never heard anything about me. I looked for your cassette and found it before you or the cops did. That ought to convince you. I won't go to meet you till after I've had confirmation from my bank."

"I'll take care of that right away. Call me in two hours, in my car. We'll decide when and where to meet."

Gorodish took out the sheet of paper on which he had written the name and address of his bank, and of the hotel where the Japanese was staying. Saporta shook his hand.

Gorodish got out and Louis, who hadn't gone far, resumed his place behind the wheel of the Mercedes.

A tan Peugeot 604 parked near the Hôtel de la Grande Chasse. Louis got out of it. After making sure there was only one exit, he sat down at the counter of a nearby café and waited. His trained eyes never left the door of the hotel.

It wasn't easy for Paulo to get hold of a big, heavy truck on short notice, but he finally succeeded and notified his boss immediately. Saporta, for once, was driving the Mercedes himself.

They had agreed to meet on a bridge over the highway. Saporta was the first to arrive. He took a few steps and smoked a cigar without going too far away from his car. Then the massive truck rolled to a stop behind the Mercedes and Paulo climbed down from it.

"I think this one will do the job," he said.

"Let's go and have a look at the road."

The place they had chosen was twenty miles from Paris. Here, the highway had only one lane on each side and was intersected by a narrow side road. The barrier down the middle of the highway would prevent the Japanese from swerving aside.

"What do you think?" asked Saporta.

"It's fine. There's not much traffic and he won't see me coming till it's too late. I'll turn off my headlights, just to be sure."

"All we have to do now is wait for Louis and Gorodish to call."

Saporta went back to his car and poured himself a shot of Scotch. Paulo moved the truck into position and rejoined his boss.

Gorodish called. Saporta told him how to get to their meeting place, then he walked to an inn. He had an urgent call to make.

The phone rang in one of the offices of the Vice Squad.

"It's me. . . . Any news?" asked Saporta.

"Not yet," answered the policeman. "That messenger keeps slipping through our fingers. But we'll get him. We know all his contacts. Sooner or later he'll make a mistake."

"I think I'm pulling ahead of you at the finish line. I know who has the cassette. If things go the way they're supposed to, I'll get it in a few hours."

"Terrific! Do you need any help?"

"No, I think we can manage by ourselves."

"This thing is making trouble for me. The big wheels know about the cassette and they want results. We have to work out something that will satisfy everyone."

Saporta was silent for a moment. Then he puffed on his cigar and said, "That should be possible. Let me think awhile. I'll be in my car. Call me later, in about two hours."

He left the inn. Outside, everything was quiet. He walked along the road and saw the truck in the distance. He breathed deeply. As soon as he had the cassette, he would take care of Nadia. He wasn't yet sure what he would do with her.

When he reached his car he still hadn't decided. He wanted to do something impressive, something that would serve as an example and be remembered a long time. There were a lot of resentful people waiting for a chance to get even with him, and they had to be shown what would happen to them if they tried it.

"Gorodish called again," said Paulo. "He says he'll be here in an hour."

"Still no word from Louis?"

"No."

Saporta went back to examine the place where the accident was scheduled to happen. He had to think of a way for the cops to come out looking good. When the police failed, reporters started sticking their noses into things, and that wasn't good for anyone.

Louis dropped a ten-franc bill on the counter. The Japanese had just come out of the hotel. Seeing him cross the street and come toward him, Louis slowed down and took time to buy a pack of cigarettes.

The Japanese passed in front of the café. He wore

glasses and walked with his body tilted forward, as if he were about to fall. Louis left the café and followed him from a distance.

The Japanese went into a caterer's shop. From the street, Louis saw him leaning over the different foods. He talked with the owner of the shop, pointing to the pâtés, the salads, the petits fours. He seemed to be taking a course in French cuisine. It was a good ten minutes before he had the owner wrap up what he had chosen. Judging from the amount of it, he was planning to give a party.

Louis saw him take out a wad of bills, pay for the food, and start back toward the hotel. On the way, he stopped to put the two packages into the back seat of a Renault 16 with Paris license plates, then he went into the hotel. Five minutes later, a bellhop came out with a suitcase and put it into the trunk of the Renault. By then, Louis had gone back to his Peugeot.

Paulo picked up the walkie-talkie on the front seat of the Mercedes. Louis was calling.

"He just left in his car and I'm behind him. We should be there in about half an hour. I'll call you back."

Gorodish parked his station wagon behind the Mercedes and joined Saporta.

"Is everything going all right?"

"So far, yes. I have to talk to you about something, Serge. I'm a little worried about the cops. I mean the ones who are on my side. We've been working together to get that cassette. They're as interested in it as I am, because it's as dangerous for them as it is for me. They want me to keep them from looking bad by finding some way for them not to come up empty-handed, you understand?"

"Yes, but the whole police force isn't working with you, and if your cops find the cassette, how do you know the others, the real cops, won't get hold of it?"

"That's the problem. I've been thinking about it and I've got an idea. Since you have the cassette, you know that messenger, right?"

"Yes. But what I'd like to know is how the cassette got into his motorbike."

Saporta rubbed his eyes and looked at Gorodish with amusement.

"It's simple. I was on the trail of the cassette from the start. One of my people gave it to a police inspector, a woman, and I followed her while she was carrying it. She wanted to hide it because she thought we were going to grab her, so when she walked past your messenger's motorbike she dropped it into the saddlebag. We didn't see her do it. But when she went back to get the cassette, the messenger had left. Funny, isn't it?"

"Hilarious. What are you planning to do for your cops?"

"They have to find a cassette. Not the one you're going to give me, of course, but another one, just like it."

"And what will be on it?"

"That's what I want to talk to you about. According to the police, the messenger loves music. Is that true?"

"Yes."

"If someone who loves music finds a cassette in his saddlebag, what's he most likely to do with it?"

"Record music over whatever's on it."

"Exactly. And that's what it's going to look like he did. Do you know what kind of music he has in his apartment?"

"Yes."

"Then you'll buy a Memorex C-60 cassette and record his kind of music on it. You'll tell him to call the cops—it doesn't matter which cops, because the message will get to the right ones. On the phone, he'll pretend he's cracked under the strain of having the police after him, and say he wants to turn himself in. He'll say he doesn't know why they're after him, but he's in his apartment now and he'll be waiting for them. The cassette will be somewhere in the apartment. The cops will find it when they get there. They'll listen to it and ask him why that music is on it. He'll say he found it and used it to record a music program. If they ask him if he heard what was on it before, he'll say he only listened to a little of it and it sounded like a recording of some kind of crime program on the radio. Can you arrange all that?"

"I think so. The cops—the ones who aren't working with you, that is—will be flabbergasted."

"The inspector who comes to get the cassette will be one of the honest cops. Only the one who sends him will know what's going on."

"I'm willing to try."

"It'll have to be done tonight. Is that possible?"

"Yes."

"All right, it's settled. As soon as the messenger is in his apartment and everything's ready, call me and I'll start things going. Now, about your Japanese. He's left and one of my men is following him. We should hear from him soon. Do you want to see the place where the accident is going to happen?"

"No, I'm sure you've done a good job of setting it up."

"Where will you give me the cassette?"

"In my car, after the accident. I'll wait for you on the road, a little farther on. You'll pass me, stop a hundred yards ahead of me, and walk back."

"You're taking precautions..."

"Isn't that how you've stayed alive?"

Saporta gave Gorodish his one-sided smile and offered him a cigar. They smoked awhile in silence, then Gorodish went back to his car. Saporta began waiting for Louis' signal.

Simon Weinstadt was a little pale. The time had come to tell Cynthia that there was a tape of her last concert. To make it easier, he had invited her to dinner at the Lapérouse Restaurant. They had just sat down at their table there. She could tell he was anxious about something. They ordered seafood.

When the champagne had been served, she asked casually, "What's the matter, Simon?"

"I don't know how to approach the subject. . . . A lot of things have been happening in the last few days."

"Things that concern me?"

Weinstadt drank half a glass of champagne, gathered his wits, and came out with it all at once: "There's a tape of your last concert. I've heard it. It's excellent."

Cynthia stiffened and her upper lip quivered. Weinstadt had the feeling she was about to scratch his eyes out.

"Who made that tape?"

"I don't know. I've only met the man who seems to own it. It's for sale."

"That's ridiculous. No one can sell my voice without my permission. I want that tape, Simon. You hear me? I want it!"

"We can buy it, if you want to, but the price would be enormous. The record companies have made big offers for it."

"But they won't buy it unless I've signed a contract with them, will they? So it's worth much less than its owner thinks."

"That's true as far as the legitimate record companies are concerned, but you're forgetting that there are more and more pirate companies, in both Europe and America. A tape like that would be a gold mine for one of those companies. They won't ask your permission to sell it on the underground market. Some of them are very rich and well organized. They put out recordings of the greatest artists. I think that if the tape isn't sold with your consent, it will be sold without it."

"Why did you get in touch with the record companies before you told me about the tape?"

"I wanted to be able to give you the final offers. It's a habit. I don't like my artists to be mixed up in the preliminary dealings."

"Well, what are the offers?"

"From DGG, a five-year recording program with Karajan, Giulini and Abbado, and an exclusive contract with an advance of however much you want."

"But what about the tape? How much are they willing to pay for it?"

"Four hundred thousand deutsche marks."

"That's an impressive offer."

"There's a problem I should tell you about. When Philips found out that DGG was taking the lead, they told me they intended to launch another black American singer, with a repertory similar to yours, who would give you serious competition."

Cynthia laughed heartily.

"Serious competition? They're dreaming. They can record anyone they want."

"Of course. You know . . ."

Weinstadt stopped short, taken aback by the change that had suddenly come over Cynthia. She stood up, furiously knocked over the champagne glasses, and strode across the restaurant to ask for her coat. She was beside herself with rage.

Her chauffeur, surprised to see her come out so soon, hurried to open the door of the black Cadillac.

"Drive anywhere! Just keep going!" she ordered.

He began driving along the Seine, feeling as if he were transporting a wild animal.

Saporta called his accomplice in the police to tell him that he would have the cassette that night, and would call back to let him know the exact time.

Gorodish waited, thinking of nothing. He was watching. His .45 automatic was beside him on the seat of his car.

Far ahead of him, Louis saw the taillights of the Japanese's car. In ten minutes he would stop on the side of the road to alert Saporta and Paulo.

The Japanese looked at his watch. A quarter to ten. Plenty of time to get to his eleven o'clock appointment with Gorodish. He sniffed the delicious smell of the food in the back seat, slowed down, and came to a stop on the shoulder of the road, at the edge of the forest. He unwrapped his packages, carefully spread out their contents, opened his bottle of Corton-Charlemagne with the corkscrew of his Swiss Army knife, and began by eating two slices of extraordinarily good smoked salmon.

Louis passed him and stopped to wait on a side road. After a few minutes, not having seen the Japanese go past, he drove back to find out what was happening.

In the glow of the Renault's ceiling light, he saw the Japanese holding a chunk of pâté in one hand and a bottle in the other.

Louis stopped a little farther down the road, turned around, and parked with his lights off.

Saporta picked up the walkie-talkie.

"He's stopped to have a picnic," said Louis. "We're about seven miles away from you. I'll call you again as soon as we start."

"Be careful. He may be up to something."

"I'll keep my eyes open."

Saporta walked to the truck and told Paulo to turn off the engine. When he heard that the Japanese was picnicking, Paulo opened his eyes as wide as saucers.

After emptying his bottle and feasting for twenty-three minutes, the Japanese neatly wrapped up the leftovers, turned off the ceiling light, buckled his seat belt, and started off.

Louis immediately sent the signal. Paulo jumped into his truck, drove it to the crossing and turned off its headlights. The walkie-talkie hung from his neck. He gunned the engine a little. It sounded good.

Three miles from the crossing, Louis speeded up, passed the Japanese, kept pulling farther ahead of him, and parked on a side road two hundred yards from the truck. He was about to give Paulo the final signal. He had to be sure he didn't report the wrong car.

Paulo had strapped himself to the seat of the truck, expecting to get a serious jolt from the collision. He kept pressing down on the gas pedal every few seconds, a little nervously.

Suddenly headlights glared in the darkness, far down the road. "That must be him," Paulo told himself. He got ready to make the short run that would leave his truck blocking the highway.

The Renault went by Louis so fast that he felt a rush of air behind it. The Japanese was driving with a heavy foot now.

Louis pushed the button of the walkie-talkie and said calmly, "Here he comes."

Paulo let the yellow headlights come closer. The Japanese saw a truck stopped on a side road at the top of a hill, apparently waiting for him to pass before turning onto the highway. He gave his car more gas to keep from losing speed on the uphill stretch.

When the approaching headlights were only fifty or sixty yards away, Paulo clutched the steering wheel, said a short prayer, let out the clutch, and pushed down hard on the accelerator. The massive truck leaped forward and stopped, cutting off the highway. There was a hideous sound of tires squealing and metal being violently crushed. The Renault was squeezed under the truck and what was left of it came out the other side.

Paulo felt as if a giant fist had knocked him sideways. He looked to his left: a shapeless mass of metal had just exploded. No use bothering to go.

and look. He was relieved to find that the truck could still move. He shifted gears without difficulty and headed for Paris, followed by Louis.

Saporta drove off behind them. He soon saw Gorodish's station wagon parked beside the road, but it seemed to be empty.

SAPORTA SLOWED DOWN AND PASSED GOROD-
ish's car. It really was empty. But he decided he would still go through with the plan he
had agreed to.

He parked the Mercedes a hundred yards down
the road, left the engine running, and began walking back toward the station wagon. With all his
senses alert in the darkness, he kept his hand on
the .38 in his overcoat pocket. There was no sound
except for the gentle murmur of the engine fading
away behind him.

When Saporta reached the station wagon, he stood
still for a few seconds, then opened the door. On
the front seat, he saw a cassette player and a cassette.
He waited awhile, thinking Gorodish might show
up. He didn't. Saporta began listening to the cassette and recognized Gorodish's voice: "Leave your
car where it is and take mine. The keys are in the
glove compartment. Leave your keys in your car and
do what I'm about to tell you. Drive two miles

toward Paris, go past a garage called the Total, and take the little road on your right."

Saporta started the station wagon and followed Gorodish's instructions.

As soon as the station wagon had disappeared, Gorodish came out of the forest with his .45 in his hand. He got into the Mercedes, turned it around, and drove off in the opposite direction from the one Saporta had taken.

Since he was suspicious, he had worked out an itinerary to make sure that neither Louis nor Paulo followed Saporta. He had switched cars so Saporta couldn't use the phone in his Mercedes. Gorodish wanted to see him alone, and that was why he had taken precautions.

While Saporta was driving along the winding road that branched off the highway, Gorodish took a much shorter route to the place where he wanted to meet him: an old water tower. From the top of it, he could watch the whole area and easily spot approaching cars.

He parked the Mercedes, got out, and climbed to the top of the concrete tower. Saporta would be there in about ten minutes.

Saporta was still following the winding road. Finally he came to a long straight stretch, saw the water tower with his Mercedes parked in front of it, and knew he had reached the meeting place.

He stopped the station wagon behind the Mercedes. Now he had to go to the top of that sinister-looking tower. He began climbing the iron stairs, being careful not to slip. He was a little out of breath when he got to the platform. Gorodish was there.

"I've done what you wanted: you have the money and I've gotten rid of your Japanese for you."

"And here's the famous cassette," said Gorodish, taking it from his pocket.

"Have you thought over my proposition?"

"For a partnership? No, I haven't changed my mind. I want to go on working alone. You can go down and make sure you've got the right cassette."

The two men looked at each other for a moment. Fierce hatred flashed in Saporta's eyes and Gorodish clearly knew what he was thinking. Saporta backed toward the stairs, still looking at Gorodish. He went down, got into the station wagon, and put the cassette on the player. Then, keeping his eyes on the top of the tower, where Gorodish had remained, he listened to the beginning of the cassette. It was the right one.

"Don't forget the cassette for the cops," he shouted up to Gorodish. "I'll wait to hear from you before I give them the green light."

"I'll take care of it tonight," answered Gorodish, also shouting. "I'll call you in your car."

Saporta got into his Mercedes and took off at high speed. He was fuming with rage. This was the first time a man had imposed his will on him. He swore he would get that bastard Gorodish some-day. But for the moment he had to finish what still remained to be done, and then he would have the pleasure of making Nadia pay for the humiliation she had caused him.

On the way back to Paris he imagined excruciating tortures for her and wondered if he could think of something better than a slow death.

Gorodish waited till the Mercedes had disappeared, then got into his station wagon and began driving to his country house. Alba and Jules must be waiting for him anxiously.

He stopped at a gas station and called to tell them to get ready to leave. Everything was finished now. Or almost finished. . . .

As soon as he was back at the Hôtel George-V, Saporta called the home number of his policeman friend in the Vice Squad.

"It's done, Boulanger. We've got the cassette."

"I've been waiting to hear from you. I couldn't sleep."

"I've arranged for you to find the other cassette."

"What's on it?"

"Nothing but music. Opera. That'll be a nice little joke, won't it?"

"Now that we've got the real cassette, I can laugh at anything."

"I'll call you as soon as the messenger gets home."

"About what time?"

"Your guess is as good as mine. He's the only problem we still have to deal with. He's heard the cassette."

This was disturbing news to Boulanger.

"Are you sure?" he asked.

"Positive. We have to get rid of him."

"I can't do it. There's been a big uproar lately about the police killing people during arrests. If I did that, on top of not getting the cassette with the original recording on it, I'd be out on my ear."

"All right, I'll do it myself. Send in your cops when I've finished."

"I'll still need to know when he gets home, to be sure they won't get there too late."

"I'll call you."

Saporta hung up. He didn't like doing the dirty

work, but this job was so delicate that he couldn't turn it over to Paulo or Louis. He would go to the apartment alone. It had been years since the last time he killed someone.

Boulanger's thoughts had been racing wildly ever since his conversation with Saporta. It had left him trembling. He had quickly begun making arrangements to fly to South America in case things went wrong, and now he was ready. He poured himself a glass of cognac. He needed it.

For the last few years he had been waiting for the monkey wrench that would sooner or later fall into the intricate mechanism he had set up with Saporta. In nine years of collaboration he had amassed an impressive fortune. He owned a magnificent oceanfront estate in South America, ready for his retirement. There, he could openly lead the kind of life that corresponded to his wealth. He had decided to ask for early retirement so he could enjoy his money longer. He had visions of himself finishing out his days, and nights, in the company of alluring and obliging women.

The only problem was Saporta. He would refuse to let Boulanger back out of their arrangement, and Boulanger knew it.

He slowly sipped his cognac. Something was sprouting in his mind. When it had taken shape he realized it was an excellent idea, though risky.

Jules and Alba had just finished locking up the house when they saw the headlights of Gorodish's station wagon shining on the weeds that bordered the unpaved driveway. They were glad he was back. Especially Alba, because she had been sure he was going to sell the cassette and she knew it would be

dangerous. She hadn't said anything about it to
Jules. They had talked a lot, but she had always
steered the conversation away from her life with
Serge.

Gorodish happily embraced them both. He had
taken a big gamble and won. The three of them
left immediately in his station wagon.

He had invented a story to calm Jules down. He
told him he had talked to the police about him and
they had agreed to forget his minor offenses if he
gave them the cassette. They would come to his
apartment to get it. After that, he would be safe.
It was the only way to get Saporta's men off his
trail. Otherwise, they wouldn't give up till they
killed him.

Jules said he would be glad to get rid of the
cassette. He was exhausted from what he had been
through. All he wanted was to get back to his
peaceful life of work and music. For the last few
hours he had been thinking of Cynthia.

"Do you have any news about the tape of Cynthia's concert?" he asked Gorodish.

"Yes. The bids have gone up to a reasonable level.
The only problem now is getting her to sign a
contract. Weinstadt is working on it."

"I hope he can convince her."

"If he hasn't done it by now, I think we can
forget about selling the tape. Unless we go to a
pirate record company."

"Do you know any?"

"We'll find some, if necessary."

Jules drifted off into his daydreams, remember-
ing the room at the Ritz and Cynthia in her red
gown.

"When we get to Paris," said Gorodish, "I'll drop

you off at your apartment and you'll wait there. Not long, no more than half an hour. The cops will come, you'll give them the cassette, and that'll be the end of it. Then we can start thinking about music again. Okay?"

"Since you think it's what I should do..."

"It's the only solution. You have to let the cops save face by pretending they found that damned cassette on their own."

They drove into Paris. Traffic was light. When they stopped in front of Jules' building, Gorodish gave him the cassette. He and Alba went upstairs with him to reassure him, then they left, promising to see him again the next day.

Gorodish took Alba to a taxi stand and handed her the keys to their apartment.

"Lock yourself in and wait for me."

"Why aren't you coming with me?"

"I still have something to do."

He kissed her, then drove back toward Jules' building. He called Saporta from a phone booth.

"The messenger is home now, you can send the cops."

"He knows what to do?"

"Yes. He's expecting them."

Gorodish parked his car on a side street, went into the building, and climbed the stairs. Instead of knocking on Jules' door, he went on up to the next floor, took out his .45, and began waiting.

Paula was in Boulanger's apartment. He had called her in the middle of the night and told her to come immediately. His plan was all worked out. Now he only had to put the pawns in place and be patient.

The phone rang. He left Paula and took the call in his bedroom.

"The messenger just got home," Saporta said in a flat voice. "Give me an hour before you send your cops."

"Be sure and do the job right, so we'll be finished with this thing once and for all."

"You can count on me."

Boulanger went back into the living room, trying not to show the anxiety rising inside him now that everything was coming down to the wire. He hoped Paula would be able to do what he expected of her.

They left in his car. The building Jules lived in wasn't very far away.

"Since you're the one who started all this," Boulanger said to Paula, "I'll let you finish it by yourself. That way, you can make up for your mistake."

"Thanks, I appreciate it."

"The messenger has broken down. He's at the end of his rope. I think you'll know how to handle him."

"I'll try."

"I'll wait for you at headquarters. People from Narcotics will be there, and all the top brass. For once, they won't have anything to complain about. I'll send a car for you. Meanwhile, I'll wake up the brass."

They stopped in front of Jules' building.

"You have your gun?" Boulanger asked as Paula was getting out of the car.

She patted her pocket in reply and disappeared into the dark doorway.

Jules didn't know why, but he was trembling with fear. He tried to calm down, in vain. The slightest sound threw him into a panic. He made himself a large cup of coffee and sat on his bed, with the cassette beside him.

When he heard the sound of a car door closing in the street below, he was paralyzed. He waited, staring straight ahead. Footsteps on the stairs, then silence. Finally someone knocked.

"Who is it?" asked Jules.

"Police. You can open the door."

He opened it and was surprised to see a woman smiling at him.

"Come in."

Paula sat down on the bed.

"Is this it?" she asked, picking up the cassette.

"Yes."

"It's all over now. There's nothing to be afraid of anymore."

"The whole thing has been crazy. I couldn't have taken it much longer."

From his car, Boulanger called in the order to assemble everyone. Then he parked a few hundred yards away, furtively walked back, and hid in a doorway facing Jules' building.

Saporta came on foot. Boulanger saw him on the sidewalk across the street. His plan was working. At last he was going to be free of Saporta, the man who had made him rich. It was a good way to end his career as a policeman. Society would be grateful to him. He didn't feel too bad about sacrificing Paula. After all, she was the one who had gotten him into this mess.

Saporta was going to kill the messenger and Paula. Then, when he came out of the building, Boulanger would kill him. That would close the circle and make sure no one ever talked.

* * *

As Saporta crept up the stairs like a cat, he took out his .38 and screwed on the silencer. He listened intently to every sound. Now and then the old wooden staircase creaked mournfully and he felt as if the silence had been shattered by a gong.

Paula heard a noise on the landing and was horrified to realize that neither she nor Jules had thought to lock the door. Too late now: the knob was already turning. She took out her gun and signaled Jules to stay where he was. Because of the entrance hall, he would be sheltered for a moment. She slipped into the bathroom, left its door ajar, and waited.

Jules was deathly pale. He slid down behind one of his Célestion speakers.

The front door was gently pushed open. Paula saw the long shape of a pistol with a silencer, then Saporta's profile.

He rushed into the room, spotted Jules' hands clinging to the speaker, and aimed his pistol at it. Just then his head exploded like a pumpkin. Paula had flung open the bathroom door and fired twice.

Several seconds went by before she lowered her gun, then she quickly took off her coat and covered Saporta's head with it. Blood and bits of brain had spattered in all directions. She saw Jules' hands still on the speaker.

He slowly stood up and let out a nervous sob. Paula took him in her arms. He was completely bewildered. He had thought the cops were in collusion with the gangsters, and now a cop had saved his life. He looked at Paula as if he were trying to find an explanation in her face.

"Why are you looking at me like that?"

"You weren't working with him?" he asked, pointing to the corpse.

"That's not a policeman. It's Saporta."

"I know, and that's why I don't understand. Saporta had the police on his side. It's on the cassette. Do you know a cop named Boulanger?"

"What!" exclaimed Paula.

"Boulanger, I'm sure of the name. He was protecting Saporta."

Paula instantly realized that Boulanger had meant to send her into a death trap.

Boulanger started. He had just heard two shots fired without a silencer. It was hard for him to believe Saporta would have taken that risk. He decided to wait a minute before going up to see what had happened. During that minute it occurred to him that maybe Paula had shot Saporta. It seemed impossible, and yet . . .

When Saporta didn't come out of the building, Boulanger knew he had to kill Paula and the messenger. Afterward, he would only have to change the order in which the shots had been fired. His story would be that Saporta had shot the two others, and that he had then shot Saporta.

He had to act fast, while Paula was still too shaky to be on her guard.

He crossed the street, pushed open the big glazed door with his shoulder, and ran up the stairs.

Paula shoved Jules into the bathroom, closed the door behind him, sat down on the bed, and pointed her pistol at the front doorway, which was still open.

As soon as a figure appeared in the shadowy rectangle, she emptied her gun into it. Expecting to take her by surprise, Boulanger didn't have time to aim. One of his bullets went over her head, then he was thrown back against the banister. She stepped toward him. He was dead, with a look of amazement on his face.

Jules came out of the bathroom.

"This time it's really over," Paula said in a toneless voice.

She called headquarters and asked them to send an ambulance and Boulanger's superior.

A few heads appeared in half-open doorways but no one dared to come out.

"You'll have to come by and see us," Paula told Jules, "so we can take down your statement and have you sign it."

"Right now?" he asked wearily.

"No, tomorrow will be soon enough. Your head will be clearer when you've had some sleep."

"Would you mind closing the door?"

Paula pushed it shut with her foot.

Gorodish was relieved. Paula had succeeded in killing both Saporta and Boulanger. Gorodish had been ready to intervene at any moment. Luckily it hadn't been necessary. It was better to let the cops manage on their own, if they could. They weren't always incompetent.

After hearing Jules' voice, Gorodish put his .45 back in his belt, came down the stairs and stepped over Boulanger's body. The four bullets had hit him in the chest and belly.

Gorodish silently left the building, walked to his car, and took out his copy of the cassette he had given Saporta. He had kept it as a life-insurance policy but he didn't need it anymore, now that Saporta was dead. He was going to give it to Paula.

He wanted to avoid the commotion that would follow if her superiors discovered that the cassette she had found was nothing but a recording of music, and having the real cassette was the only way she could justify what she had done. As a side benefit, it would put Saporta's men behind bars, including Louis and Paulo.

Now he had to get it to Paula without letting Jules know. He went back into the building, came out a few moments later, walked to the nearest phone booth, and dialed Jules' number.

Paula answered.

"Who is this?"

"It doesn't matter. The cassette you found in Jules' apartment isn't the one you want. Is it in your pocket?"

"Yes, but what..."

"Leave it there. Go down to the lobby of the building. In Jules' mailbox you'll find another cassette, the real one. Don't tell him about this, and hurry, because there's no lock on the mailbox."

Gorodish hung up. Paula heard police sirens in the distance.

"I'll only be gone a minute," she told Jules, walking to the door.

She found the cassette in the mailbox and went back upstairs.

"What was that all about?" asked Jules.

"The call was from my headquarters. They wanted me to pick up something downstairs. I'm sorry, but I can't tell you what it was. Official business."

He shrugged.

"Do you want another cup of coffee?"

"Yes, thanks. But first, play the cassette for me. I'm anxious to hear it."

She handed him the cassette she had just taken

from the mailbox. He put it on his player and Nadia's deeply moving voice began her story.

Paula told herself that someone had really done her a tremendous favor. She couldn't imagine who he might be or why he had done it, but she had the right cassette and that was what mattered.

"You can turn it off now," she said. "I just wanted to hear how it sounded."

"It sounds depressing to me."

Paula took back the cassette.

A regiment of cops and high police officials were climbing the stairs.

"We'll clean up all this," said Paula, pointing to the blood. "It'll be better if you don't stay here. Do you know a place where you can go?"

"Yes. Can I make a phone call before I leave?"

"Of course. You won't forget to stop by tomorrow, will you?"

"No, I'll remember."

She wrote her name and address on a slip of paper.

"Come straight to my office. Just give them your name and they'll let you in."

"Okay."

"Make your phone call and get out of here. It's not going to be pleasant to look at. You'll have to leave me your key. Do you have an extra one?"

"No, but it doesn't matter because I won't come back till after I've seen you tomorrow."

They exchanged a tired smile. The room was already full of people. The routine work had begun.

Jules picked up his phone and ordered a taxi. Paula went downstairs with him to wait for it.

The cops listened to the cassette. As they heard the names of Saporta's accomplices, they gave orders to arrest them. Some long vacations were about to begin in the underworld.

* * *

The taxi rolled along calmly, as if nothing had happened. The sky had cleared and the world was making a new start. Soon it would be dawn. Jules was sprawled out in the backseat. Life seemed beautiful to him. His mind was filled with a single image.

CHAPTER ELEVEN

WHEN *GORODISH* CAME HOME, HE FOUND a telegram: CALL ME ANY TIME. WEIN-STADT. Gorodish was tired. Even so, he called the impresario.

"What's happening?"

"I'm afraid our plan has been shot down. I told Cynthia about the tape and it made her furious. We'll never get her consent. I'm in a spot where I have no room to maneuver: if I say one more word about that plan to her, she'll leave me, and I can't afford to lose an artist like her. So I'm bowing out. All I can do for you—and she suggested this herself—is to buy the tape in her name, but I doubt that the price would interest you."

"Let me think it over and call you back when I've decided what I want to do. Can you give me an idea of how much she'd be willing to pay?"

"Fifty thousand francs, at the most."

"You're right, that's probably not enough to interest me. But I'll call you tomorrow anyway."

Gorodish couldn't help smiling. He liked Cynthia Hawkins' stubborn determination not to make any recordings. As he was about to rejoin Alba, he heard the buzzer of the intercom. It was Jules. Gorodish unlocked the door for him.

Jules came in, looking dazed, and gave a rapid, disorderly account of the night's events. Gorodish reassured him. The whole thing was finished now.

Jules sat down in the reclining chair.

"My place is a mess. They're cleaning it up. I have to get some sleep. Can I stay here?"

"Sure, no problem."

"Let's have some breakfast," said Alba, who had just walked into the room. "I'm hungry."

The three of them went to the kitchen. The table was soon loaded with cheese, bread, jam, coffee, and eggs. They were all famished.

It was past dawn now. The daylight hurt their tired eyes.

"I talked to Weinstadt about the tape," said Gorodish. "Cynthia's furous and he's terrified. She refuses to sign a contract with a record company but she's offered to buy the tape. I like that. It's original."

Jules nearly choked.

"You're not going to sell *her* the tape, are you?"

"I didn't say I was. I just said she'd offered to buy it. Anyway, the tape is yours. You're free to do whatever you like with it."

"We agreed to be partners. If you have another idea...But we can't sell it to her."

"We tried to bring off a big deal and we failed. It's too bad, but that's how it is. At least we have the satisfaction of seeing someone turn down a big contract with DGG that must include a gigantic advance. You have to admit that's worth something.

And I meant what I said: you can do whatever you want with the tape. All I ask is that you let me listen to it once in a while if you keep it."

"Serge, you're fantastic."

Alba was eating a huge piece of Roquefort. The two men seemed funny to her, with their tape.

"What *are* you going to do with it?" she asked Jules.

"I don't know. I'll think about it when I've had some sleep."

"That's a good idea," said Alba, "let's go to bed."

She stood up, kissed Jules and Serge, and disappeared.

Gorodish gave Jules a sleeping bag. Jules put it on the sofa in the living room and crawled into it. He had earned his tape, thought Gorodish.

Serge undressed and spent a good twenty minutes under a hot shower while his mind emptied itself of everything that had happened in the last few days.

He went into his bedroom, where he had the last shock of the night. Alba was lying in his bed.

"I can't sleep. Let me stay with you."

He didn't answer. He knew he had been a little hard on Alba and himself. This time he decided to let himself go. He lay down beside her. She was naked. He felt her warm, vibrant body next to him, and kissed her. Her lips were so soft, so fragrant . . .

She looked at him with an angelic smile.

"You know you're the one I love, don't you? Jules is just a friend."

Since Serge didn't want to start a conversation that would tarnish those magic moments, he let his lips take hers again. He felt her tremble. She put her arms around him and pressed herself against him with all her strength.

* * *

It was a little past four o'clock in the afternoon when Jules woke up. He took a shower, shaved his three-day beard, tried some of Serge's cologne, and ordered a taxi.

When he arrived at the entrance of the Ritz, he was panic-stricken at the thought that Cynthia might have left for London.

Not daring to go straight up to her suite, he called from the reception desk. The sound of her warm voice on the phone made his heart pound wildly. He ran up the stairs, because it was faster than taking the elevator, and arrived out of breath.

Cynthia kissed him on both cheeks and stroked his forehead.

"I've been terribly worried. What happened?"

"It's so incredible I don't know where to start. Anyway, it's over and I understand everything now. If you want me to, I'll tell you all about it later, from the beginning."

"I'd like to hear about it. But I have a rehearsal this evening with Geoffrey, my pianist. He's back from Germany. The director of the Opéra is letting me use the main auditorium. Because some of the unions are on strike, I can use it all evening."

"I wish I could go there. . . ."

"You know I never let anyone hear my rehearsals," said Cynthia. He seemed so dismayed that she added, "No one but you."

Jules was ecstatic.

"Are you free now?" he asked.

"Yes, for the next two hours."

"Will you let me take you somewhere?"

"If you like. I'll call the chauffeur."

Jules enjoyed seeing the bellhops hurry to open doors for them.

They got into the big black Cadillac. He felt as if he were in a living room with Cynthia's divine odor floating in the air.

"Where are we going?" she asked.

"Rue de l'Université."

The Cadillac glided along like a shark, without the slightest sound. She took his hand. They looked at each other and began a silent conversation. It suddenly occurred to him that he had come very close to dying without having known this moment.

"This is where we stop," he said.

The chauffeur opened the door. Jules had taken the keys to the apartment, so there was no need to wake up Serge and Alba.

Just riding in the elevator with Cynthia seemed to him one of the most beautiful experiences it was possible to have.

He showed her into the living room after taking her black mink coat.

"Sit down in that chair," he said.

She obeyed, intrigued.

"This is a nice apartment. Whose is it?"

"It belongs to some friends of mine."

Cynthia was wearing a white silk scarf. Jules took it and gently tied it over her eyes. She said nothing. He saw her smile.

He went to the tape player that he had already prepared and turned it on.

The first notes of the piano were immediately followed by the voice.

Cynthia pulled off the blindfold and leaped to her feet. Jules was frightened. She stood several seconds with her eyes flashing, but she still said nothing and he sensed that she was beginning to listen. She sat down again and kept looking at him till the end of the Schubert lied. When the applause broke out, she motioned him to stop the tape.

"How did you get that tape, Jules?"

He evaded the question. "It's for you. I'm giving it to you."

"You mean it's the original?"

"Yes, and there's no copy of it."

She thought for a few moments.

"Are you the one who recorded it?"

"Yes," he said timidly, apprehensive about what was going to happen next.

She went on looking at him. Her expression was mysterious to him. He couldn't tell if she was going to slap him or throw herself in his arms.

Finally, after what seemed to him a very long time, he thought he saw her smile.

"Let me hear the rest of it," she said.

She heard the whole concert. It affected her strongly. This was the first time she had ever listened to herself.

"You're really giving it to me?"

He put the tape into its box, kissed it, and handed it to her.

"Come," she said, "it's time to go to the Opéra."

They got into the Cadillac again. She seemed unable to speak. When they came to the Place de la Concorde he felt the fur of her coat slide across his shoulders and neck. She pulled him closer to her and held him in her arms till they reached the Opéra.

It was hard for him to get out of the car. He felt as if he had smoked a dozen joints.

A very elegant young man was waiting for them at the stage door. He nodded to Jules and kissed Cynthia's hand.

"The director is in a bargaining session with the

union leaders. He's asked me to give you his apology for not meeting you in person. If you'll come with me, I'll take you to the stage. Your pianist is waiting for you there."

Jules sat down in a seat that he judged to be at the ideal distance from Cynthia.

Her voice arose, extraordinarily pure, and filled the auditorium. He recognized a Schumann lied. His whole body quivered. Sometimes Cynthia stopped, said a few words to Geoffrey and started over.

She was singing for Jules alone and he knew it.

After a long rehearsal, she repeated one of the Schumann lieder she had worked on with Geoffrey, then told him that would be all for tonight and kissed him on the cheek. He pointed to Jules, who was still floating in a blissful trance.

Cynthia went backstage and saw the elegant young man coming toward her.

"Have you finished, Miss Hawkins?"

"Yes, but I'd like to ask a favor of you."

"Please do."

"Can you turn off all the lights in the auditorium except the ones that show the Chagall ceiling? For years I've dreamed of being able to look at it for a long time, alone."

"I'll be glad to do that for you, Miss Hawkins. Stay as long as you like, and call me on extension 312 when you want me to come for you."

Cynthia gave the young man her most charming smile and went into the auditorium.

Jules was startled when the lights went off. He heard a door close. In the red velvet silence, he dimly saw Cynthia coming toward him.

She had draped her coat over her shoulders. The soft light from the ceiling gently enveloped her. Incapable of uttering a sound, Jules went forward to meet her.

She put her hands on either side of his face and guided his mouth to hers. He felt himself melting into a warm universe that drew him toward its center. This must be heaven, he thought. Maybe he was dead, killed by a bullet, and everything happening to him was part of the afterlife.

Cynthia's coat dropped to the floor and Jules found himself lying on it with her, as if it had pulled them down in its fall. Then her face briefly disappeared behind her white silk dress as it unfurled like a breaking wave, leaving her dark body stranded on the fur of her coat.

Jules' clothes had somehow left him. Cynthia's body, nebulous in the shadows, was no longer separated from him. Suddenly he had the feeling that the auditorium had turned upside down. The sky was a symphony of pure color, a radiant background against which appeared Cynthia's face, neck, and shoulders while she made love with him for a long time, almost without moving, as in an endless dream.

That night, Alba lay looking up at the ceiling with a serious, contemplative expression on her face.

Serge came into her room, still looking ecstatic from having just played two dozen Bach preludes and fugues.

"Are you sulking?" he asked gently.

"No, I'm thinking."

"About Jules?"

"You're jealous," said Alba, without really believing it.

Serge sat down beside her, kissed her on the temples, and caressed her forehead.

"Tell me what you were thinking about," he insisted.

"The Mona Lisa. I'd like to have it in my room."

"I'll buy you a reproduction of it," he said, disappointed.

"No. I want to steal the original."

"No one can accuse you of not being ambitious. . . . I read somewhere that the Mona Lisa is really a picture of a man."

"It doesn't look like a man to me."

"Maybe it's not true. Do you have any other plans?"

"Not right now. I'm fed up with small-time jobs. I want us to do something really fantastic, something that will go down in history."

"We'll think about it," said Serge. "I'm sure we'll get an idea. You and I were meant to do great things together."

About the Author

Delacorta is the pen-name of Daniel Odier. Born in Geneva, Switzerland, in 1945, he studied painting in Rome, received his university degree in Paris, and worked as music critic for a leading Swiss newspaper. His first book, THE JOB: *Interviews with William Burroughs*, was published in the U.S. in 1969. Since then, he has written seven novels under his real name, including the recently filmed LIGHT YEARS AWAY and BROKEN DREAMS. Publication of DIVA will be followed by more Gorodish and Alba novels: NANA, LUNA, and LOLA.